# Fire Consumes Us

## A. R. HELLBENDER

A.R. Hellbender

This book is a work of fiction. The characters, incidents and dialogue are drawn from the author's imagination and are not construed as real. Any resemblance to actual events or persons, living or dead, is entirely coincidental. No manticores were hurt in the making of this book.

Fire Consumes Us, Copyright ©2024 by Katherine Boyce. All Rights Reserved. Printed in the United States of America. No part of this book may be used or reproduced in any manner whatsoever without written permission from the publisher except in the case of brief quotations embodied in critical articles and reviews. Copies may be purchased for educational, business, or sales promotional use. For information, contact the publisher.

First Edition

Cover Designed by Halie S. Williams

Library of Congress Cataloging-in-Publication Data has been applied for.

ISBN-13: 9798344928333

Published by MAЯS Publishing, Vancouver, WA
First Paperback Printing - December 2024

Published in the United States of America

Fire Consumes Us

Dedicated to anyone who has found themselves torn between two places, no matter what that means to you.

A.R. Hellbender

Fire Consumes Us

## ACKNOWLEDGMENTS

There were many years between the time that this book was finished and the time I chose it as my next published work, and several people who made it possible then, now and in the time in between. My mother for a lifetime of exposure to the culture she came from. My dad for continuing to inspire me to write and for his tireless work as the main editor. My aunt Jackie for continually mentioning this book over the past several years and asking me if it would be published. My husband Jay for his encouragement. Sorry this book isn't about a time traveling indigenous people from the arctic circle, honey.

    I would also like to thank David Pipgras of MARS Publishing for doing the work of getting this book published. And my good friend Halie Williams for the incredible cover art.

    Lastly, I want to thank the many Iranian authors out there, especially the ones who showed me that you can be half Iranian like me and still write stories based on a culture you're part of.

A.R. Hellbender

## CHAPTER ONE

It was time for the manticore to choose. If one could call it choosing, for a manticore always knew who they were looking for when the time came.

If the stinger on the great cat's tail, and the bat wings, went unnoticed, as if they could, a manticore would seem like simply a black lion. But anyone in Hashem would know what they were looking at when they saw one.

Sniffing the night air, the manticore spread her wings and flew up into the highest room of the house, perching herself onto the windowsill. Creeping through the room and into a hallway, she knew where to go. She hardly even needed to peek into the individual rooms before she found the human child.

The child was not yet three years old, but she stared at the manticore, unafraid. She even smiled as she reached one hand out to pet the big cat's nose. She hardly seemed to notice being stung by the manticore's tail.

Immediately, her curls blackened, and the round pupils in her brown eyes became slits in green irises. But she was young enough that she would not notice the difference when next she looked in the mirror. Her parents would, no doubt, and they would know what it meant.

The manticore turned from the room and left. She knew they would meet again.

Ydana awoke from the dream. It was the same one she had most nights. The one that reminded her of her earliest memory, of meeting the manticore. Never sure if the dream represented the real event as it had truly happened, or if she was imagining it based on what she was told, she simply ignored it upon waking up.

"Ydana, are you awake?" Her maid, Niusha, was knocking on the door.

"Yes," Ydana groaned. She never got a moment to herself.

Niusha entered. "Come, child, you must dress for breakfast. It would not do to keep your lady mother waiting."

With a sigh, Ydana drew the bed covers aside and got up.

"Mother can wait as long as she likes."

Reluctantly, Ydana suffered through letting Niusha dress her, as she usually did. Once her clothing was in order, Ydana looked into the mirror as Niusha began braiding her black hair back into several braids. Usually, Ydana's mother insisted that her daughter wear a hat to cover her dark hair as much as possible, so that it would not shine the red-black of a manticore's coat quite so obviously, but it was hardly seemly to wear a hat to breakfast.

Though Ydana knew that her odd hair and cat eyes upset her mother, and even her father when he was home, she saw no reason to be ashamed of it. So what if she became a manticore one day? She would still be able to turn human again at will, if the legends floating around her city were anything to go by.

Once she was completely dressed, Ydana joined her mother at the breakfast table, where a plate of bread and cheese awaited her. Ydana sighed again. What really sounded like good food was steak, whether it was cooked or not. But her mother had forbidden the consumption of meat in the house. Anything to discourage her daughter from becoming a manticore. As if there was a way.

At the opposite end of the table sat her mother. Lady Ylaine Blanchard had blonde hair tied up into a loose bun. A few strands escaped, giving her face a less severe look, yet the wrinkles at the corners of her mouth were evidence of a woman who frowned too much. Lady Ylaine had supposedly been a happy woman once, when she had traveled to Hashem from Grusrecia, her young son Victor in tow, and fallen in love with Azra Veshteh. If Ydana's father hadn't been a cousin of the Podishah, she doubted that Lady Ylaine would have even looked at him twice. But if the portraits in her father's study were anything to go by, her parents had truly loved each other once. But Ydana could hardly connect those happy portraits with the frowning woman who sat before her now.

"You're late," was all her mother said.

"I'm terribly sorry, mother," Ydana pulled out her chair and sat down. She stared down at her plate of bread and vegetables.

Lady Ylaine did not speak for several minutes as she cut each bite even smaller before consuming it. She hardly looked at Ydana, as usual.

"Ydana, eat your breakfast," Lady Ylaine finally urged her. "There will not be much time to eat later, and you do not want to be too hungry during the ball."

Ydana groaned, which her mother rewarded with an angry glare.

"Do I have to go to the ball?" Ydana asked.

Lady Ylaine rolled her eyes before turning back to her breakfast.

"Of course you have to go. The ball in honor of Lord Warrington's birthday is the event of the year. I'm willing to bet that even the Podishah will be there, what with him being such good friends with Lord Warrington. And it is important that you meet Lord Warrington's younger son, Sasha. Do you remember him? According to his mother, he has shown somewhat of an interest in you. This may be your one chance to make a good life for yourself."

Lord Warrington was one of a handful of other Grusrecian nobles who had traveled to Hashem, either as ambassadors or because Hashem was the fashionable place to be, despite the occasional manticores.

Ydana finally gave up picking at her meager breakfast and dropped her fork onto the plate with a clatter.

"Mother, I hardly want to get married now. I don't want to be treated like I only get one chance at anything just because of what I am."

"You are going, and that is final," her mother said sternly.

Walking behind her mother, Ydana pulled on the itchy sleeves of her dress. At least her mother had not insisted she wear a hat this time, for once, so she did not complain. The last time that Ydana had been to a ball was two years prior, when she was only 14 and had spent the time sitting outside with other children. Her manners had not mattered then, and the hat had been acceptable. But this time, her mother had deemed a hat unseemly for a sixteen-year-old.

Behind them, their carriage departed back towards home, leaving Ydana with no way back from here. In front of them, more people were on their way inside, their invitations collected from them by the doorman.

Lady Ylaine drew two invitations from her handbag, for herself and Ydana, and handed them to the man, who nodded.

No sooner had they gotten inside, than a middle-aged man turned from another guest to approach them.

"Lady Blanchard," he spread his arms wide in a gesture of welcome. "How nice that you have arrived."

"Thank you kindly for your invite once again, Lord Warrington," Lady Ylaine smiled her fake smile. "Azra would have loved to be here as well, but he is away. Teaching Victor to conduct business, you understand how it is. I have instead brought my daughter."

"Lovely to see you again, Ydana," Lord Warrington smiled at Ydana.

"You know my name?" Ydana could think of nothing else to say.

"But of course," Lord Warrington laughed as Lady Ylaine gave Ydana a stern glare.

On the other side of the room stood a girl nearly Ydana's age, who appeared to be the only person in the room other than herself who had black hair with a reddish tint. And her long hair was down, almost to her waist, as of she wasn't hiding her manticore nature in the least. Though there were plenty of other Hashemi in the room other than Ydana and the stranger, she still stood out, making Ydana wonder why no one else had noticed a manticore in their midst. Or perhaps they had, and none of them wanted to be the one to confront her.

She did not look away when Ydana saw her, but instead did not show any expression. It was as if she were not used to making face expressions at all. And instead of wearing blue or green like most everyone else, her clothing was all black.

"Ydana, you should go say hello to Sasha," Lord Warrington drew her attention back to the conversation. "He just went outside to the courtyard."

With a nod, Ydana left them, trying not to look backwards at the stranger, despite feeling her eyes on her back.

Upon getting to the courtyard, Ydana found herself taking a deep breath of fresh air. Being in a room with such a large crowd of people had felt too stifling. She had needed to be out in the open. There were a few people outside, but only two or three turned to look at her when she entered, as they were too busy admiring the garden.

It was easy to spot Princess Zahra, the Podishah's own daughter, who was surrounded by several people all waiting for a chance to speak to her. Zahra had hardly changed at all since she and Ydana used to be made to play together until they were nearly thirteen.

Even when Zahra had begun to have her doubts about having a manticore for a playmate, she had still tolerated Ydana, and never made her feel left out. But, like any friendship Ydana had ever had, it did not last. The older they grew, the more reservations Zahra had about spending any more time with a manticore than she had to, thinking that Ydana would turn at any time.

Now, in the garden, Zahra looked in Ydana's direction with only the barest hint of recognition on her face, before turning to speak to someone else. Though Ydana had barely given Zahra a thought since they had ceased to be friends, she suddenly found herself missing what they had once had.

"Ydana?"

Ydana turned around to face the speaker. She had expected, almost hoped, that it would be the stranger she had seen inside, but it was not.

"Sasha?" Ydana was not entirely sure if the young man who stood before her was Sasha, for it could also have been one of his two brothers. She had met each of them only a few times, but Sasha was her own age and had spent time with her when they were children.

"It is nice to see you again, and without the ridiculous hat that your mother makes you wear," Sasha smiled.

Ydana had nearly forgotten the incident four years prior, when she had taken her hat off to play tag with some other children, and faced her mother's wrath for it. Sasha had told her since that he felt sorry for making her take her hat off. He had not thought that her mother would be so upset with her.

"She thought it would seem silly for me to wear a hat to a ball at my age, and of course I agree," Ydana said.

"Will you walk with me?" Sasha held out his arm.

Taking his arm, Ydana went with him into the garden, which was illuminated only by the light from the house and a few lanterns that hung in the trees.

"How are your parents?" Sasha asked.

"They are well," Ydana looked at the flowers instead of at him. "Father is away again, as usual. What about your family?"

"My oldest brother is getting married soon. My mother dislikes his fiancée, but I'm sure she will get over it."

A young girl approached them, holding a hairpin in her hand.

"Excuse me, miss, but I think you dropped this."

Ydana had not even noticed that one of her hairpins had fallen out.

"Thank you," she bent to take it from the girl, when another woman appeared, who was probably the girl's governess.

"Don't speak to her!" the governess began dragging the child away. "Do you see her hair? Remember what your mother told you!"

"Excuse me," Sasha let go of Ydana's arm, "being a manticore is nothing to be ashamed of. She did not choose to be what she is, and she is a person like you or me."

With one angry look at Sasha, the governess grabbed her charge by the arm and hauled her away.

"Thank you," Ydana looked at Sasha. "No one has ever stood up for me before."

"It was no problem. It all just disgusts me, how manticores are treated. You have black hair, so what?"

"Black hair that shines red in the light, catlike eyes, an appetite for meat," Ydana listed the attributes that made her a manticore. "And I often can't sleep at night."

"But have you met the one who turned you into a manticore? Have you become one yourself and flown off somewhere?" Sasha asked, knowing the answer. "You're still human, too."

Ydana could not help but smile.

"I have never told you," Sasha offered her his arm again as the two continued walking. "I had a younger brother once. I was only seven when he became a manticore, but I knew the signs. My parents could not afford the scandal of it, so they shipped him off to a boarding school in Grusrecia, small as he was, and stopped speaking of him. It was not long before the boarding school sent a letter to my parents, informing them that he had disappeared."

"Did he turn into a real manticore early, then?" Ydana wondered. "What happened?"

"That's what I am guessing, but there is no way to know for sure. Either way, I felt terribly for him, the way my parents shipped him off like he was a racehorse for sale. Perhaps he would still be here if they had kept him at home."

"I'm sorry," Ydana said. "That's terrible."

"Sasha," one of Sasha's brothers was coming to meet them. "Father requires your assistance."

"Alright, I will be right there," Sasha turned to Ydana, "I'm sorry, Ydana, but I need to go. I hope we see each other again soon."

Once the two were gone, Ydana began wandering around the garden on her own. Having hardly eaten since her small breakfast, she felt her stomach growling. Before long, a rabbit darted out of the bushes and into the path in front of her.

Despite herself, Ydana let out a low growl, which made the rabbit shiver. The rabbit was fast as it sprinted up the path, but Ydana was faster. In one leap, she overtook the rabbit. It continued to struggle, but one swift bite to the neck made it grow still.

Beyond the rabbit in her hands, Ydana noticed, was a pair of boots. Looking up, she saw that the boots were on the feet of a woman. The same Hashemi stranger who had been staring at her from across the ballroom. Ydana could not help blushing as the manticore woman stared down at her.

"You should try to eat before such events. That way, your hunger won't get the best of you when you are trying to appear human."

"I *am* human," Ydana's mouth was full of rabbit flesh as she struggled to devour the rabbit before anyone else would see.

"Are you? Do humans usually have blood all over their clothing?"

Ydana dropped the rabbit. Blood all over her clothing? She stared down at the front of her dress, which was covered in a smear of rabbit blood. What would her mother say this time?

"Come with me," the stranger held out her hand.

Following the stranger to the perimeter of the garden, Ydana's worry vanished. No matter how bloody her dress was, she would figure something out.

Once the two exited through an opening in the tall shrubbery that encircled the garden, the stranger turned to Ydana. As dark as it was outside, she could see that this girl's pupils were slits in green irises, just like hers.

"Your humanity may be valuable to you, but you cannot hide forever."

Though she wanted to protest, Ydana knew that she was right.

"What are you doing here, then, if you're embracing your manticore nature?" she could not help but ask.

The stranger snickered. "I was always a manticore. After 50 years of roaming the forests alone, my mother found a small boy and stung him, turning him into what you are. A human on the verge of becoming a manticore. Once he became a manticore for good, he joined her in the forest. The two of them had one cub, which was me."

"You're the one who stung me, aren't you?" Ydana lowered her voice. "That's why you're here."

The stranger nodded.

"But why did you turn me into a manticore? Why not find another manticore?"

"There were once only two manticores in the world, from which all others who have been born manticores are descended. Most manticores are related to each other in some way, and there are not very many of us. Therefore, we can only choose our mates from among the humans."

Ydana stepped backwards.

"Is *that* why you stung me? Just so that you could have another manticore to have a manticore cub with? That won't even work if we're both girls anyway!" Ydana realized that she was screaming. "You ruined my life! I could have had a normal life, without the shame, if you had left me alone!"

"Calm down," her companion said. "It's not like that."

"What *is* it like?"

"We don't simply choose a house to walk into and sting whatever child we find," her companion explained. "We are guided by our instincts. I stung you not because you were the child I happened to find in that room, but because you were already going to be someone I could get along with. Someone who would prefer the forest to your meager townhouse. Stinging someone who does not fit those qualities kills them."

"Well, you still ruined my life," Ydana turned towards the garden entrance.

"What are you going to do about the blood?" the stranger called after her.

Ydana had forgotten about the blood on her dress. She turned back around to face her companion as she changed shape. As she got down to all fours, bat wings grew from her back and a muzzle from her nose. Once she gained her lionlike form, she twitched the stinger on the end of her tail. With one more glance at Ydana, the black lion turned and ran through the field. Ydana watched until she was far enough away to spread her wings and fly.

Entering the garden, Ydana was surprised to find a group of nearly ten people crowded around a bush. With a jolt, she realized that that was where she had left the half-eaten rabbit.

One by one, the people turned to face her. One was the governess from before, who shielded the young girl behind her back.

"It must have been her," the governess pointed. "I saw her in the garden earlier."

"Look, she has blood on her dress," someone else was also pointing.

Not waiting for anything more to happen, Ydana turned and ran back through the entrance and out into the vast field beyond.

"Get her!" someone was shouting. "Quickly, before she transforms!"

"I'm sorry, mother," Ydana muttered to herself as she ran. "I'm sorry, Sasha."

She noticed a moment later that she was running on all fours. She was also taller. Flapping her new wings, feathered instead of batlike like the other manticore's had been, she took off into the sky.

Not looking back at her pursuers, she flew farther up, feeling the wind in her mane.

After hours of tearing through the night sky, Ydana realized that she had nowhere to go but home. She doubted her mother was home yet, but, not wanting to take a chance, she flew to her own bedroom window and perched onto the windowsill before swinging her now-human legs through the window and climbing inside.

## CHAPTER TWO

"You've certainly done it now," Ydana's mother stomped through the front door, handing her cloak to the maid.

Ydana did not look up from her uneaten plate of salad. She had avoided her mother all morning since the incident at the ball.

"Lord Warrington won't allow his son to marry you now, I'm afraid," her mother continued, angrily.

"What difference does it make, mother?" Ydana threw her salad fork onto the table. "He already knew that I was a manticore. In fact, the whole city already knew. Why decide that I'm not worth marrying his son simply because I've finally transformed into a manticore, when they already knew I was going to eventually."

Lady Ylaine sat herself down at the table, opposite Ydana. Surprising herself, Ydana met her mother's eyes, not backing down.

"People prefer things to be out of sight, out of mind, Ydana," Lady Ylaine looked slightly taken aback at her daughter's cold glare, but recovered her composure. "You could have married an Earl's son if you had only gone another few months to a year without transforming, at least not so publicly. But now there's little hope that you will make a good marriage at all."

"Perhaps I can do something else, then," Ydana surprised herself yet again by speaking up. "I could go out on business like father and Victor."

"No one would take you as seriously as they do your father and brother, I'm afraid," her mother scowled. "At least not back home in Grusrecia where much of the business is conducted. Not only because you're a girl, but because you're a manticore."

It was the first time her mother had used that word out loud in a long time, and Ydana shuddered.

"And even if they did, that does not excuse you from making a marriage that would benefit this family," her mother continued. "In any case, I have invited Lord and Lady Warrington, as well as Sasha, to tea tomorrow. Please do all that you can to persuade them to let Sasha marry you, or else we may have to send you to boarding school."

"Boarding school?" Ydana stared at her mother in shock.

"At least until the scandal dies down," her mother clarified. "I'm afraid that our family's reputation has suffered quite a blow after last night, and it may even affect your father's reputation among his business associates."

Without another word, Ydana got up from the table and ran up the stairs to her room.

Slamming the door behind her, Ydana finally allowed herself to cry. As silent tears streamed down her face, she stepped towards the window. She hated her mother for caring about their reputation, she hated Sasha for saying that manticores needed to be treated better but not doing anything to help her now, and she hated the manticore who stung her, because she should have left her alone. But most of all, she hated herself.

Being partly human and partly manticore was too difficult a curse to bear. And if the manticore she had met at the ball was right, it was her own fault that she had been stung. But if that were true, was there someplace else where she would be happier?

Before she knew it, she was jumping out the window on four legs, spreading her feathered wings wide. She flew around the night sky, around a few of the floating islands that humans did not get to explore. She came to land on the largest one she saw, which was empty of wildlife except for an owl, who stared at her without fear.

The islands that floated in the sky above Hashem were mostly very small, but she had heard that there was a large one somewhere that was said to be home to manticores. Surely that would not be one that lay so close to the city, but she felt the need to check, all the same. The floating islands moved around, after all. It was unknown what sort of magic kept the islands afloat, but they were said to have come from far to the north, where they had risen from the ground due to some sort of magic. Surely if she were able to fly from island to island now that she had gained the ability to fly, being a manticore had to have some benefits.

Jumping back into the sky, she flew the rest of the way to Lord Warrington's mansion. Seeing no sign of Sasha, she flew to the border of Hashem, where the Rostami mountain range stood tall. Perching herself onto the tallest, snowiest mountain, she let loose a mighty roar that shook the ground.

Flying up into the sky again, she turned back towards home. On the way, she saw a deer running through a clearing. Diving down, she pounced onto the deer before it even knew she was there. Tearing into its flesh, she let its blood run down her face. Having eaten her fill, she tore upwards once more. Before she had flown very high, she heard several people shouting. She heard the word 'manticore' and knew that she had been spotted. Flying higher and faster, she blended in with the night sky.

Dawn was breaking as she spotted her house. Perching onto her rooftop, she watched the sun rise before swooping down into her bedroom window and landing on her bed, human once more.

Hearing a scream, she looked up. Niusha, standing up from a chair in the corner, covered her mouth.

"It's true," Niusha's voice was barely above a whisper. "You're a…"

"This is hardly news, Niusha," Ydana narrowed her eyes. "You knew I was a manticore. What are you doing here, anyway? It can't be time to get dressed."

"Your lady mother wanted me to stay here and keep an eye on you," Niusha nervously smoothed her mousy brown hair. "When you weren't here, I was hardly going to go down and tell her that you were gone, so I waited for you to come back. Forgive me, my lady, I hardly expected you to come back looking like…"

"It's alright," Ydana stole a glance towards her mirror and was surprised to find blood all over her face from the deer she had eaten. Fetching a cloth from the closet, she wiped the blood off as best she could and lay down to sleep. Before sleep took her, she heard the door open and close as Niusha hastily departed.

Ydana slept later than she had intended to, and was loathe to get out of bed to bathe and dress. Niusha, who still helped arrange Ydana's hair into neat braids, seemed afraid to touch her, and said nothing at all. Though the silence was somewhat awkward, Ydana was glad not to hear any commentary from Niusha about the visit from Sasha and his parents.

When it was nearly time for Sasha and his parents to arrive for tea, Ydana was almost as nervous as her mother was. But while her mother paced endlessly and barked at the maids, Ydana sat at the table, perfectly still, not uttering a word. When a knock sounded at the door, she nearly jumped.

"Get up, Ydana," her mother hissed, and Ydana hastily stood from her chair just as the butler opened the door. "And remember, not one word out of you."

She heard the voices of Lord and Lady Warrington. Perhaps Sasha had not come with them after all. Ydana would have breathed a sigh of relief had her corset allowed her to do so. But when Lord and Lady Warrington turned the corner into the sitting room, Sasha followed after, looking straight at Ydana before deliberately avoiding her glance.

"Lady Blanchard," Lady Warrington greeted Ydana's mother. "How wonderful to see you. And Ydana, you've grown so much since last I saw you. I didn't see you at the ball, I'm afraid."

The mention of the ball made Ydana step backwards in surprise. Across the room, Sasha looked equally uncomfortable.

"It's nice to see you, as well," Ydana could think of nothing else to say. She had never remembered meeting Lady Warrington, just as she had not remembered Lord Warrington at the ball.

"Let's sit down and have tea," Lady Ylaine waited until their guests sat down before taking her seat.

Ydana was the last to sit, taking her place on the chair next to her mother's. A maid poured the tea for each of them, and Ydana looked down at her tea, where the reflection of her bright green eye stared back at her.

"I know what you have invited us here to discuss," Lord Warrington skipped the small talk. "And unfortunately, I am firm on my decision not to allow Sasha to marry anyone but a nice polite girl from a good family. I am aware that Ydana is nice and polite, but that is not all she is."

"I was hoping," Lady Ylaine smiled politely, "that perhaps you would reconsider your decision if Ydana could…control herself. I assure you that the incident at the ball was the one and only time that Ydana has ever…turned. And she sticks to a strict diet of fruits and vegetables in order to remain in control."

Ydana forced herself to remain silent. A family that shipped their son to boarding school to keep him from becoming a manticore would surely have tried the same things that Ydana's own mother was doing to keep her human, and would know that it didn't work. Staring into her tea, she reminded herself that this conversation was more about her mother being satisfied that she had tried everything, than about actually being able to convince Sasha's parents to let him marry her.

"I assure you we have thought of everything," Lord Warrington stirred sugar into his tea. "Our Sasha truly did want to marry your daughter, and did not change his mind even after the incident at the ball. But we cannot allow it. If something similar were to happen again, even a decade from now, our family cannot afford the scandal."

Looking up, Ydana met Sasha's gaze. He looked apologetic as he looked from her to his father.

"But Ydana's father is cousin to the Podishah," Lady Ylaine protested. "Surely Sasha would want to marry into royalty."

"While we did consider that fact," Lord Warrington said, "I have more of the Podishah's favor than your family does. If Sasha wanted to marry one of the Podishah's daughters, I'm sure he could do so."

"There are a few reasons why a human should not marry a manticore," Lady Warrington picked up where her husband left off. "Firstly, a manticore has a longer lifespan. It's difficult to say exactly how much longer, but the odds are that Ydana will age much more slowly than Sasha."

At this, Ydana's mother stole a glance at her daughter, as if only realizing for the first time that she was a different sort of being altogether.

"Secondly," Lady Warrington continued, "a manticore stung Ydana when she was a child. When he did so, he was choosing her. What's to stop this manticore from stealing her away one day? It would not look good to have the wife of one of our sons simply vanish. The fact that Ydana transformed at the ball most likely means that she has recently met the manticore who stung her."

As Lady Warrington rattled off fact after fact about manticores, Ydana found herself wondering how this woman knew so much.

"Is this true?" Lady Ylaine demanded of Ydana. "Have you met another manticore?"

Ydana shook her head. She knew that her mother could tell if she lied, but all that mattered was giving the answer that her mother wanted to hear.

"Do you see?" Lady Ylaine turned back to Lord and Lady Warrington. "She hasn't met another manticore. She has been here at home in the days leading up to the ball, and ever since then."

"I'm so sorry, Lady Ylaine," Lady Warrington sipped her tea. "I know it seems a bit harsh of us not to allow Sasha to marry the girl he chose, but we have had our dealings with manticores in the past, and had to work very hard to bury all of that."

Lord Warrington's gaze darted towards his wife.

"And we cannot afford for that to happen again," Lady Warrington finished. "In fact, you may want to consider burying your secrets as well."

Ydana stared, shocked, at Lady Warrington. She saw that Sasha was also staring at his mother, a shocked expression on his face.

"May I speak to Ydana for a moment?" Sasha set his tea cup down.

"Of course," his father answered.

Standing up from their chairs, Ydana and Sasha left the room. Her hands shaking, Ydana led Sasha through the foyer and into her father's study. Shutting the door behind them, Ydana turned to Sasha.

"I'm so sorry about all of this," Sasha began. "You don't deserve any of this humiliation at all."

"It's hardly your fault," Ydana wished he would just get to the point so that he and his parents would leave.

"Did you meet the manticore who stung you? Was he at the ball?"

Ydana nodded.

"What did he look like?" Sasha asked. "I don't think I saw him."

"I don't know," Ydana was not sure how to describe the manticore she had met. "She looked about our age, and she was wearing all black. No different from the way I would have expected a manticore to look."

"She? How is it possible for a female manticore to sting a girl?"

Ydana had no answer.

"In any case, I don't care that you're a manticore," Sasha continued. "In fact, I somewhat envy you your ability to fly, and your longer lifespan. If it were up to me, I would still choose to marry you, because I don't think our differences matter. But there's no way my parents would allow me to now."

"But they knew I was a manticore before," Ydana pointed out. "What changed? I was always going to transform sooner or later."

"I don't know. Perhaps they didn't believe it, or weren't really going to allow us to marry. But listen to me. If there's nothing I can do to change my parents' minds, I still hope that you find happiness. You're just as deserving of that as anyone. I have a feeling that my parents are going to recommend sending you to boarding school."

Ydana could only stare at him. Though her mother had mentioned boarding school before, Ydana had never seriously thought of that as a possibility. And she shuddered to think that it could be a boarding school in Grusrecia, a country that she had never even visited. Hashem was her home, and she did not want to leave.

"And if that does happen," Sasha placed both hands on her shoulders, "please look out for yourself. If you have to disappear like my brother did, that's alright, too. If a manticore comes for you, just go with them. Be free."

To Ydana's surprise, he kissed her full on the lips. Gasping in surprise, she could do nothing but place her hands on his arms. Pulling away from her, he only looked at her for a moment before heading for the door.

"And if you ever meet my little brother, Leon, among the manticores, let him know that I love him, and that I'm still thinking about him," he opened the door, not looking back towards her.

"I...I will," Ydana whispered.

She gave him a moment to leave, before following him back to the sitting room, where they both stood a short distance from the door instead of entering.

"I do think boarding school is your best option," Lady Warrington was saying from inside. "Most boarding schools have had manticores before, especially in Hashem, and they may be able to help her."

Ydana and Sasha exchanged a look.

Her mother's reply to Lady Warrington was nearly inaudible. It sounded as if the two women were sitting closer together than they had been before, whispering to each other. No doubt Lady Warrington was comforting her mother.

As soon as Ydana began wondering if Lord Warrington was still in the same room, someone behind her cleared their throat.

Ydana and Sasha spun around to come face to face with Lord Warrington.

"You hardly need permission to enter your own sitting room, Ydana," he looked from her to Sasha. "And Sasha, haven't we taught you better than to listen to other people's conversations?"

"I'm sorry, father. I didn't…hear anything."

Ydana suspected he had been about to say 'I didn't mean to' but knew that his father would smell the lie.

"Let us fetch your mother and head home," Lord Warrington made his way into the sitting room.

Once the small party gathered in the foyer and Niusha brought the Warrington's cloaks to them, Lord and Lady Warrington bid Lady Ylaine farewell. Lord Warrington did not address Ydana at all, and his wife only smiled awkwardly at her. Ydana said nothing, her face expressionless.

Waiting for his parents to don their cloaks and leave, Sasha turned to Lady Ylaine.

"Thank you very much for the tea," he said, before turning to Ydana. "I hope to see you again soon, Ydana."

His eyes met hers only briefly before he left to follow his parents. Ydana stared after him as he donned his cloak, pulling the hood over his head. As soon as the butler shut the door, blocking Sasha from view, Ydana turned to her mother.

"Don't send me to boarding school, I beg you."

"Nothing will be decided for sure until your father gets home," Ydana's mother said sternly. "And any boarding school we send you to would be one of the best there is, I promise."

Without a word, Ydana turned away towards the staircase.

"Where are you going, young lady?" her mother called after her.

"To my room," Ydana continued up the staircase.

"I have not dismissed you."

"I apologize, mother," Ydana said snidely. "I wasn't aware that I was a servant."

"Come back down here," her mother demanded.

Reluctantly, Ydana descended the stairs to stand in front of her mother.

"Have you met another manticore?" Lady Ylaine asked.

Ydana had forgotten all about that aspect of their earlier conversation, and had not prepared herself for the possibility of her mother asking such a question. She could only nod, seeing as her mother had known she was lying earlier.

"Where?" her mother demanded.

"At the ball."

"When?"

"In the garden," Ydana was not sure what sort of information her mother was after, but she was determined to give her as little of it as possible.

"Was it the manticore who stung you?"

"How would I know such a thing? May I please go to my room?"

Dismissing her with a gesture, her mother turned away.

## CHAPTER THREE

Ydana slept for the rest of the afternoon, and awoke that night to fly through the sky once more. This time, she tore through the forest in search of prey. She caught a few rabbits, which she devoured in only a few bites, before catching a deer and biting into its throat to kill it. Instead of eating it on the ground where she risked being seen, she carried it upwards to one of the floating islands above the city.

"It seems you're getting the hang of things," came a voice behind her as she ate.

Jumping onto her four legs, she turned. The manticore she had met at the ball stood before her. She was halfway between human form and lion form, with a human head, arms and torso on top of a lion's four legs like a lion centaur, batlike wings folded behind her. Her human half was naked save for a meager piece of cloth as a shirt, and her arms were more muscular than her clothing had made her look the last time Ydana had seen her. Her long black hair was blowing in the wind.

"This is simply one of the forms we are able to take," she explained. "You will figure out how soon enough. The ability to fly while also carrying weapons or supplies can come in handy sometimes. But transforming while keeping your clothing can be difficult if you're wearing too much."

"How did you know I'd be here?" Ydana took her human form, still poised over her kill.

"It's not difficult," the manticore also took her fully human form. She remained mostly shirtless, but was wearing pants and boots. "These floating islands are the natural home of our kind. Of course, the main one we actually live on is much bigger, but these small ones do just as well for a short stay."

Ydana crouched lower over her kill as the manticore stepped forward.

"Get your own!" she growled.

"Don't worry, I'd never take anything from you. In case you hadn't noticed, you're larger than I am in our true forms."

She hadn't noticed. Of course, she had only seen the stranger in her manticore form once, and from a distance at that.

The manticore ran to the edge of the island, reverting back to her true form as she leapt off of the side. Ydana ran after her, peering over the edge as her companion soared into the forest, impressive batlike wings outstretched. She emerged almost immediately with a dead deer clutched in her forepaws. Swooping past Ydana, she landed on the ground and sank her teeth into her kill. Reverting to her own manticore form, Ydana returned to her own kill and followed suit.

"Why do you have bat wings when I have feathered ones?" Ydana turned human once she had finished eating.

"Your feathered wings are due to your being a human turned manticore. Any of our kind who was born a manticore has leathery wings like I do."

Ydana came to sit beside her companion, looking out over the edge of the floating island, towards the mountains.

"I'm surprised you haven't tried to convince me to come with you."

"Come with me where?" the manticore made no move to sit closer to her.

"Wherever manticores go."

"Ah. Well, I'm hardly going to make you go anywhere with me if you would rather stay here in your human realm," she deliberately looked away. "When last we met, it seemed as if you wanted me to leave you alone, so I did."

"Until now," Ydana began undoing her messy braids and smoothing out her hair.

"Aye, until now. But someone had to keep an eye on you, Ydana."

The use of her name surprised Ydana. She hadn't realized that the manticore even knew her name, or even thought of her as a separate person beyond simply a human she had turned into a manticore.

"What's your name?" Ydana asked.

"What do you mean?"

"You know that my name is Ydana, so what should I call you?"

The manticore in human form opened her mouth wide and let out a series of roars. Ydana nearly fell backwards, having hardly expected such a loud sound to emerge from someone in human form.

"Is...that can't possibly be your name." Ydana peered at her.

"Aye, it is." The sliver of light from the rising sun glinted off of her bright green eyes.

"That's not even a name," Ydana could hardly imagine trying to pronounce such a name, or even differentiating it from any other sound a manticore made. How would she ever meet other manticores if she wouldn't be able to keep their names straight?

"Maybe not to your human ears," she smirked.

"What's my name in your language, then? Can you translate a human name into…whatever you call that?" Ydana dared her.

Opening her mouth, she let out a roar that, surprisingly, sounded like 'Ydana'.

"Alright, tell me your name again," Ydana leaned forward, as if that would give her any hope of listening more closely.

The series of roars that the manticore pronounced sounded just as loud and jumbled as they had before.

"Sorry," Ydana looked back towards the sunrise. "I still didn't get that. I suppose I'm hopeless."

"You can call me Val. That's what my friends call me."

"Val," Ydana repeated. It sounded nothing like the series of roars that had been her true name, which made her wonder if she had made it up entirely.

"And you're not hopeless. Don't ever say that," Val smiled. "You'll get there. Understanding manticore-speak takes practice. You wouldn't have survived my sting if you had been just another human, unable to take being a manticore. This is who you were meant to be."

"Who I was meant to be," Ydana laughed through her nose. "A manticore."

"You're controlling yourself better among your human companions now that you've been hunting at night, haven't you?" Val finally moved closer to her.

"Just because I'm somewhat understanding what being a manticore is like doesn't mean I want to…be in some kind of relationship with you," Ydana stood up. "So don't get any ideas."

"Oh, I know that," the grim satisfaction shown in Val's voice. "Though my choosing you means that we would get along, that you never would have been happy as a human, that comes with no true guarantee that we're…romantically compatible."

"It doesn't?" Ydana turned around to face her.

"Of course not," Val stood up, facing her. Her face was still close enough to hers that their noses nearly touched. "You're not the only one I've stung, after all. Just my favorite."

Ydana's eyebrows drew together. She wanted to wipe the arrogant smirk off of her face.

"Oh, good, so you're not counting on me to find you attractive," Ydana smiled crookedly. "I'm relieved. I was worried about hurting your feelings."

"Were you really?" Val's lips were nearly touching hers. "I'm touched by your concern. I didn't think you cared."

"Well, we manticores need to look out for each other, as you said," Ydana felt a blush creep to her cheeks. She tore her gaze away from Val and stepped towards the edge of the floating island. "The sun is almost risen, so I need to make my way home. I hope we meet again soon."

Leaping off of the edge, she soared through the sky in her manticore form, not sparing Val another glance.

No sooner had Ydana risen from bed in the late morning, than Niusha appeared at her door.

"Your lord father and lord brother have arrived," the maid did not meet her eyes.

"Are you still afraid of me?" Ydana asked.

"I..."

"Never mind," Ydana rolled her eyes. "Don't bother. If I scare you, I'll do my hair myself."

Closing the door on Niusha, Ydana went to her closet and donned a gown that she could lace up herself, and braided her hair into one braid and secured it up with a hair clip.

When she came to the staircase, she peered below at her family members in the foyer.

"We came as soon as we heard," her father was saying, his voice laced with concern. "Is it true, Ylaine? Has our daughter turned?"

"I'm afraid so," her mother answered.

"Well, I'll not have it," her brother, Victor, took off his cloak and practically threw it at one of the maids. "This family has enough to worry about. We've avoided scandal thus far, and I will have nothing ruining my engagement to Elvira. Nothing!"

"Now, Victor, you needn't be so crass," her father put a hand on his stepson's shoulders. "This is your sister we're speaking of, so be polite."

Ydana wanted to laugh. Victor had never been polite to her in the least. She could not recall even one good memory of her brother, for he had always treated her as something disgusting. Any time he brought friends to the house, he either made sure she stayed out of his way, or, failing that, he would call her a freak in front of his friends, and they would all laugh at her.

"My sister, is she?" Victor sneered. "Well, I insist we avoid the scandal the best we can, and send her off somewhere out of the way."

"Or perhaps you stop treating me like an animal," Ydana descended the staircase, "and had some common decency for once in your life, Victor. You will never be rid of me, so you had best get used to my presence."

All three of her family members stared up at her with shocked expressions. None of them were used to her acting confident in the least.

"Apologies, sister dearest," Victor's words were laced with sarcasm. "I only meant that we should send you off to school where you can develop some semblance of manners. You have never been particularly normal, after all."

"Children, please," Lady Ylaine said hesitantly. She was not used to using the term 'children' in reference to the adults who were her offspring. "This is hardly the time for arguing."

"Your mother is correct," her father said. "We need to sit down and discuss what is best for this family."

Ydana was tired of hearing the phrases 'this family' and 'our family', because what it really meant was their reputation, which, it would seem, was more important than she was.

"Well, I will not sit quietly and let you all discuss my future without me," Ydana placed her hands on her hips. "I'm not a child."

Victor made to utter a retort, but was shushed by a look from his stepfather. The family moved to the sitting room while a maid brought them tea. Most of the conversation at first was Lord Azra and Victor being filled in on the events of the ball as they had truly happened, for the story had changed somewhat by the time they had heard it where they were. Victor had to be told to keep quiet several times, as he appeared to have an insult for Ydana at every turn.

"So the vegetable diet is clearly not working," Victor said snidely. "Ydana will eat from the garden, but it's the rabbits she prefers, not the plants."

"Do be quiet, Victor, and let your father and I finish speaking," Lady Ylaine turned back to her husband. "Ydana says that's when she met the manticore who stung her."

"So you do have marriage prospects after all, do you, sister?" Victor laughed.

"It's not like that," Ydana rolled her eyes at her brother. She wanted to let him know that Val had stung other people and was clearly not a marriage prospect, but she knew that Victor would only turn her words around and mention that even a hated manticore was out of her league.

"Victor, if you can't keep quiet, leave us," Lord Azra scolded his stepson.

"Lady Warrington recommended sending her to boarding school," Lady Ylaine continued. "She says that most schools have had manticores there before and can help."

"Help how?" Lord Azra asked. "I want Ydana to be taken care of, but it would hardly do to let her be unhappy. If a boarding school will give her some sense of belonging that she does not get here, perhaps that would be good. After all, we can't allow anyone who would hunt a manticore to get ahold of her."

Ydana could only stare at her father. She had never heard of anyone hunting manticores.

"Hunt a manticore?" Lady Ylaine was just as surprised. "Who would do that?"

"I have learned many things while out on business, Ylaine," Lord Azra said. "With how much Hashem has suffered in trade and tourism, due to the manticores dwelling primarily in our kingdom, there are those who hunt them. No one has been able to locate the island on which the manticores primarily live, but many have been trying for quite some time now, and I fear it is only a matter of time. I would rather Ydana be safe. And if she is known to live here, it may be best if she spent some time someplace else, where nobody knows where to look for her. Perhaps even in Grusrecia."

Feeling very cold all of a sudden, Ydana sipped her tea. It did very little to warm her up.

"What do you think of that, Ydana?" her mother looked at her. "Wouldn't you rather be safe someplace else?"

"I know I'm hated," Ydana looked down into her tea, "but I never thought anyone would want to hunt me."

"Then isn't boarding school the best option, for the time being?" her mother asked.

"I don't want to leave Hashem," Ydana protested.

"Then perhaps there is one within Hashem," her mother said. "A school close by would surely have had more manticores attending, after all."

Ydana said nothing, though she knew deep down that she would be the only manticore regardless of what boarding school she attended.

"If you're unhappy there, we can always find a different solution," her father chimed in. "But for now, it may be safest."

The last thing Ydana wanted was to leave, especially to go to a boarding school that probably had strict rules about being out at night or eating messy food. But her only other option was to leave with Val, which would only put her in danger if there were manticore hunters about. Val would undoubtedly be safer on her own than with Ydana following her around.

Unable to meet her father's eyes, Ydana nodded.

"That sounds best."

## CHAPTER FOUR

Lord Azra was able to secure a place for Ydana at the Meacham Academy for Young Women within a week of their family conversation. Until she could depart for school in another week, Ydana had promised her parents not to venture outside, provided they did not stick to the vegetable diet and instead brought her raw steak for at least one meal each day instead. At Victor's insistence, she ate her steak dinner in the kitchen, only eating breakfast and lunch with her family.

She did not so much mind this compromise, unless Victor had a friend or two over for mealtimes, which was at least every other day now that he was only recently returned from his business venture. Because of this, Ydana was quick to excuse herself from the table at most meals, and, when eating her steak in the kitchen, stayed there until Victor's friends left.

One day, as she was fetching a book from her father's study, it just so happened that one of Victor's old schoolmates was arriving at that very moment. When Victor greeted him, Ydana practically dove back into the study.

"Has your sister grown fur and claws yet?" his friend laughed. "I heard there was an incident at Lord Warrington's ball, but I wasn't there to see it."

"Unfortunately, yes," Victor replied. "That was indeed my sister who transformed at the ball. Mother and father are even feeding her raw steak now, like an animal."

"I can hear you," Ydana stepped out of the study.

Victor's friend, who Ydana now recognized as Samuel Barton, whom she had once fancied, looked surprised to see her. Ydana was equally surprised to see him, though she did not show it. Only two years prior, she had been heartbroken when Samuel made fun of her along with Victor and his other friends. In the time since, she understood that it shouldn't have been a surprise to her that a Grusrecian would make fun of her for being a manticore. Manticores were something that every Hashemi knew of, even if they had never seen one, but weren't part of Grusrecian culture.

"Well, we weren't discussing anything that's any sort of secret," Victor did not look surprised in the least that Ydana had overheard. Perhaps he had been counting on it.

Ydana briefly considered transforming right then and there, which would surely scare Victor and ensure that he would never bother her again. But she knew that if she did, if anyone in her family saw her in her manticore form, it would be back to the vegetable diet for her, and she would lose all progress she had made with gaining her family's acceptance. None of these people knew what a fearsome creature a manticore truly was, especially close up.

"I'm sure that being as immature as you have been is very impressive to your friends and Elvira," Ydana knew how much Victor valued his upcoming marriage. "So if you think your behavior towards me will help your reputation, then by all means, carry on. I'm sure Elvira would love to wake up to a ferocious beast eating dead bloody rabbits in the middle of her bedroom."

"I'll tell father to put bars on your window," Victor's face grew red. "And then I will tell the *boarding school* to put bars on your window!"

"That would do no good," Ydana smiled. "Manticores are very strong. And I'm not the only one roaming around this part of Hashem. The other manticores I know will continue to torment you. Or you could simply stop bothering me for one more week, until I leave for school. Now that sounds much simpler, doesn't it?"

"You…" Victor tried to come up with a vile enough insult before giving up and turning to his companion. "Let's go to the garden, Samuel."

No sooner had the two men departed, than Ydana burst into tears and ran upstairs to her room, where she flung herself onto the bed.

Once night fell, Ydana looked up to find Val sitting on the windowsill. Though she was wearing boots, Ydana saw that they left no dirt on the white windowsill, as if they had never touched the ground.

"Val," she sat up. "What are you doing here?"

"I came to look in on you," she said. "When we didn't meet again, I wondered if something had happened to you."

"What are *you* still doing out hunting when there are manticore hunters about?" Ydana pulled her inside, off of the windowsill, and drew the curtains shut behind her.

"There have always been manticore hunters about, ever since there have been manticores," Val stood close to her, gently placing her hands on her arms. "I'm not afraid of some humans."

"You will be if they catch you!"

"Is that the only reason you haven't been out hunting anymore?" Val smiled her roguish grin as she looked into Ydana's eyes. "Because you're afraid of being hunted? And here I wondered if you were avoiding me."

"I'm also afraid of you being hunted because you're trying to help me," Ydana yanked her arms from Val's grasp and stepped back. "My father says there are those who are searching for the island that the manticores live on, who think they are close to finding it."

"They aren't."

"You said that too quickly," Ydana said. "You can't know that for sure. I'm going to boarding school to lay low for a time, and not give the manticore hunters any reason to look for me. I suggest you also stay where they have no chance of finding you."

"I'm touched by your concern," Val's voice showed a hint of skepticism. "But humans have hunted manticores since the first two manticores roamed the kingdom. Before Hashem even had that name. I have survived nearly a century thus far, and I'm certainly not expecting to be hunted now."

Ydana was surprised at the mention of Val's age, and wanted to ask about it, but she also knew that satisfying her curiosity was the least of her worries.

Fire Consumes Us

"You have survived this long because you didn't have dead weight like me to deal with. And because you were careful, which you are not being right now by coming here."

"Very well, then," Val seemed to have run out of arguments. "I will leave. But please tell me you're alright, and that you're…eating enough."

"My parents have agreed to give me raw steak every day, and will most likely continue to do so as long as I don't do anything too out of the ordinary for a human. If you stay, you can have some. I can tell them I want to eat in my room."

"Thank you, but I will be fine," Val turned towards the window. "I can just eat your brother."

"There are several reasons not to eat my brother, no matter how horrible he is," Ydana gave Val a horrified look.

"I'm not serious," Val smirked. "Humans taste terrible."

"Please tell me you didn't find that out from firsthand experience," Ydana raised an eyebrow at her.

"Of course not. Any manticore would have to be starving to eat a human."

Another thought occurred to Ydana.

"How did you know I had a brother, and that he would be worth eating? Have you been spying on my family?"

Val breathed deeply as she turned towards the window.

"I wouldn't quite say I've been spying. But this is not the first time I've stopped by your dwelling, you are correct. I heard your brother and his friend talking outside the other day, saying things about you that made me want to rip their tongues out."

Ydana was not entirely sure whether she wanted to know what Victor and whichever friend was visiting that day were saying about her this time. Particularly if the mere thought of it was enough to make Val angry at them.

"And I must say, Ydana, that I am so sorry you have to bear being insulted," Val turned to meet Ydana's eyes again. "I had no idea what your situation was like, and I am sorry I stung you."

"That was a long time ago," Ydana stepped towards her. "You're forgiven."

"Am I really?" Val seemed genuinely surprised as she wrapped her arms around Ydana.

"Of course. As you said, it was a long time ago," she couldn't help but embrace her in return, Val's body surprisingly warm against hers.

No sooner had Ydana finished her sentence, than a knock sounded at the door.

"Lady Ydana?" came Niusha's voice. "Who are you talking to?"

Ydana froze in Val's arms.

"Nobody," she said with a grimace. She knew her voice sounded like she was smiling, which would certainly make her lie more evident. "Just myself."

"It's time for dinner," Niusha opened the door and stepped inside.

Removing her arms from around Ydana, Val scrambled to the window quicker and more silently than she had ever seen a human move, barely rustling the curtain as she hid behind it.

"I'll eat in my room today, if that's alright," Ydana sat on her bed. She could feel the sweat beading on her forehead as she wondered if Niusha had seen Val.

"I will let your lady mother know," Niusha looked around the room, even going so far as to glance underneath Ydana's bed. "Are you sure you weren't talking to somebody?"

"Who would I be talking to?" Ydana wanted to add that no one had come over, as Niusha had most likely seen, but was afraid that anything she said would only seem more suspicious.

Without answering, Niusha slipped back into the hallway. Once the sound of Niusha's footsteps faded, Ydana went to the window and drew the curtain aside, only to find that Val had gone.

## CHAPTER FIVE

The carriage ride to the Meacham Academy for Young Women was long and incredibly boring. Ydana tried to concentrate on the book she was reading, but continued to stare out the window, hoping for some sign of Val. At the same time, she hoped not to see her, as it would be too dangerous for her to fly around during the day if there were manticore hunters nearby. She hoped that she would see her again soon, that the way she had left without so much as a goodbye was not the way she would leave things forever.

Next to her, Lord Azra was bent over his own book. The cover did not have a title on it, but Ydana had glimpsed the spine of the book briefly during the ride, and noticed the word 'Manticore'. What was her father doing reading about manticores?

"Don't look so anxious, Ydana," Lady Ylaine said from the seat across from her. "The Meacham Academy is bound to be exciting. I hear their library is grand. And think of all of the friends you will make. It has been quite some time since you made friends with young ladies your own age."

"You mean she's never made friends with young ladies her own age," Victor sneered from his seat across from Lord Azra. "Not since Zahra, who was practically forced by her mother to continue spending time with Ydana. That isn't very likely to change now. Other young ladies will be just as afraid of being eaten as they always have been."

"Victor, honestly!" Lady Ylaine turned to her son. "Can you go even one hour without insulting your sister?"

"Yes, if she's not in the room," Victor said.

"Victor, we only agreed to let you come along to visit Lady Elvira because you agreed to behave," Lord Azra looked up from his book. "If you can't hold up to your end of the bargain, you will have to remain at home the next time we make this trip."

Though the Meacham Academy was run by people in Grusrecia, they had several locations, and this one was within Hashem, but close enough to Grusrecia that only another hour's ride would bring them to Victor's fiancée. Ydana was glad that she would be dropped off at the academy before they reached Elvira, for she had no desire to meet anyone who her brother admired in the least. But unfortunately, this also meant that Victor would spend the entire ride to the Meacham Academy insulting her.

Ydana's family made a few stops along the way to eat, fill their water flasks in the river, and allow the two carriage drivers to switch off. By the time they were nearing their stop, Ydana had fallen asleep.

It was dark when she awoke. Looking out the window, she saw a shadow obscure some of the stars for a moment, and wondered if it was Val. She rubbed her eyes and looked again, seeing nothing else unusual. It was more likely to be a bird, or perhaps her imagination.

The carriage pulled up to a large mansion built in the Grusrecian style, with small rectangular windows with only a simple band of gold trim. Having grown up in Hashem and never visiting her mother's old home, Ydana was used to seeing differently shaped windows with colorful patterns, complete with torches in between each one if they were on the ground floor. This Grusrecian building was illuminated by only kerosene lamps, and very few of them at that.

"We're here," Ydana's mother said as the carriage came to a roundabout and stopped before the door. The two carriage drivers got out to open the doors for Ydana and her family.

"You must be Lord and Lady Veshteh," a woman came out, holding a lantern.

"Yes, and this is Ydana." If Lady Ylaine was annoyed at the use of her husband's surname as her own, she did not show it. "And my son, Victor."

"I'm pleased to meet you all," the lady's gaze did not linger too long on each of their faces, until she came to Ydana, who had little doubt that she was looking at her green cat eyes that shone in the dark. "My name is Martina Wickham, one of the directors of the program here at Meacham Academy."

Miss Wickham hardly looked as old as Ydana would have expected someone in charge here to be. Her brown hair had no grey in it that she could see, and the freckles that adorned her face made her look even younger. Ydana had heard that most Grusrecian women of a certain social standing used powder to hide their freckles, but evidently not all did.

"I apologize for our tardiness," Lady Ylaine was saying. "We had to make a few stops along the way."

"That's quite alright, Lady Veshteh. We have prepared rooms for all of you to spend the night. If you leave your carriage there, I can have your things brought up shortly."

Letting her family members follow behind Miss Wickham first, Ydana lingered by the carriage for a few moments before taking a deep breath and entering the house after them.

"We have a few guest rooms here on the first floor," Miss Wickham whispered to Ydana's parents. "But Ydana may as well get settled into her own room upstairs."

A girl dressed in a nightgown appeared on the stairwell. The candle in her hand illuminated the scowl on her face.

"Charity, what are you doing out of bed?" Miss Wickham asked the girl.

"I came down for a drink of water," Charity said in a tone that implied that it should have been obvious. Ydana doubted the girl was there for a drink of water at all.

"After you get your drink of water, would you please show Ydana where she will be staying?"

"Of course, Miss Wickham," Charity did not bother to hide her irritation at the request.

"Thank you," Miss Wickham turned back to Ydana's family, guiding them from the room.

Unsure of what she was supposed to do, Ydana followed Charity into the kitchen and watched her pour herself a glass of water. She barely looked at Ydana before heading back up the stairs. Feeling awkward, Ydana followed her.

"You're hardly the first manticore we've had here," Charity pronounced the word 'manticore' as if it were something disgusting. "So don't assume you're special."

"Special?" Ydana could hardly imagine why her condition would be anything to be happy about. "Why would you say something like that?"

"I'm only letting you know that we all follow the same rules here. Don't go around stinging anyone, or eating anyone. In fact, stay away from the other girls altogether."

Ydana could only roll her eyes. If the other girls were all like Charity, Ydana certainly *would* stay away from them.

"That's your room," Charity hardly looked as she pointed to an open door and immediately went across the hall to a room where three other girls sat laughing together on a bed. Ydana watched as Charity joined her friends and closed the door behind her.

Just as Ydana was about to turn towards her own room, a movement made her glance down the hall. A girl was silhouetted at the other end of the hall, her eyes briefly glowing in the dark, before she disappeared into one of the rooms.

Shuddering, Ydana went into her own room. She almost thought about following the other manticore, for she had never met another who, like her, was a human turned manticore. But the late hour combined with the fact that Ydana had not seen exactly which door the girl had gone through, made her hesitate. It was better to be patient, and talk to the girl when she had time.

Her room was bare except for a bed, a desk, an empty bookshelf, and a kerosene lamp, complete with a few matches sitting next to it. Because of her manticore eyes, she could see extraordinarily well in the dark and would hardly need the lamp unless she was reading.

Taking the chair from the desk, she placed it by the window and sat down. Looking up at the sky, she saw a shadow block out a few of the stars for only a moment. Immediately, she unlatched the window and stepped up onto the windowsill. Changing into a manticore as she jumped from the window, she flew up into the sky.

She hadn't realized how much she missed the feeling of the wind in her mane, and the scent of the cold night air as she flew up to where she had just seen what had to be a manticore.

Once she was high enough up to see the surrounding area, Ydana looked around her and saw nothing, least of all another manticore. Dismayed, she floated down to the ground, wings outstretched. It had to have been her imagination. Val would hardly want to come all the way out here just to see her again, especially now that Ydana had outright said that she had no feelings for her. Now she had risked being seen in manticore form for nothing.

Movement from the corner of her eye caught her attention, and she turned her head to see a mouse running into the trees at the edge of the Meacham Academy's field. She had not yet glided to the ground before she pounced on the mouse and devoured it in one bite. Having not hunted in nearly two weeks, she felt invigorated by the taste of blood in her mouth.

The next animal she saw was a pigeon, and she killed it with one bite, gripping it in her mouth and flying with it back to her window. Human once more, she jumped down from her windowsill, the dead bird still in her mouth.

A knock sounded at the door, and Ydana hastily shoved the dead pigeon into the desk drawer.

"Come in," she called, wiping her face in case there was any blood on it. As the door opened, she kept her face turned towards the window, still afraid of any blood on her face being seen.

"Ydana, we've brought your things up," Miss Wickham opened the door.

"Thank you," Ydana kept her eyes on the window, scanning the sky for dark shapes as she heard someone behind her set her trunk down just inside the door.

It was only a moment before the door closed again, and Ydana crossed the room to where her trunk and handbag lay. Opening the trunk, she brought out a nightgown and changed into it. She had brought only clothes that did not require help lacing up, with the exception of one gown, at her mother's insistence. Lady Ylaine had wanted her to have at least one nice dress just in case of a special event, saying that any new friends she made could help her put it on. As if she would make friends, the way things were going.

When she still did not feel tired, she brought the dead bird out of the desk drawer and, laying it onto the floor, changed into her manticore form and devoured it, making sure to eat the bones as well, for fear of them being discovered later. Human once more, she checked to make sure that her nightgown showed no traces of blood before she began unpacking the books she had brought, and arranging them onto the bookshelf. That done, she made herself lay down in bed until she finally slept.

It was too early when a knock sounded at the door.

"Ydana, it's time to wake up," Miss Wickham's voice sounded.

Ydana sprang from her bed and went to the door. "Is it possible to sleep just a bit longer?"

"I'm afraid not," Miss Wickham greeted her with a tentative smile. "That's not allowed unless you're sick. Do you need any help getting dressed?"

Ydana shook her head and shut the door. Changing her clothes and brushing her hair, she opened the door only a minute later to find Miss Wickham still waiting for her, and followed her downstairs in silence.

"Did my family already leave?" Ydana was unsure of whether she hoped they had, or not.

"They're about to," Miss Wickham ushered her past the dining room where the other girls were sitting down to eat, out to the hallway.

Her parents stood in the hallway, talking to a grey-haired woman who was dressed much more neatly than Miss Wickham. Ydana guessed that she was the one in charge.

"There are fewer students here than at the other Meacham Academies we have," the grey-haired woman was telling Ydana's parents. "Most people don't want to send their children to Hashem, for fear of a manticore turning them. But even if we do close this location, it would not be until every one of our students is of age or otherwise leaves us. After all, each of the Grusrecian girls here have their reasons for being here rather than at our other locations. Many of their parents are living in Hashem. We also have two Hashemi students here, so Ydana should feel right at home."

Ydana's parents looked over the grey-haired woman's shoulder at Ydana, making the grey-haired woman turn as well, and fall silent as her eyes landed on Ydana. Slowly, she stepped away from Ydana's parents, allowing them to say their farewells.

"Have a good time visiting Lady Elvira," Ydana was the first to speak.

"We will be back this way on the return to Hashem, in a few weeks," Ydana's mother said.

Fire Consumes Us

"Don't forget to write," her father stepped forward and embraced her. "Be safe."

"I will," she returned her father's embrace.

"Miss Wickham, will you show them out?" the grey-haired woman said as Ydana's father stepped back to stand with her mother. "Ydana, let us go to breakfast."

To Ydana's surprise, the woman placed a hand on her shoulder, which Ydana fought the urge to shake off.

"My name is Mrs. Moon," the grey-haired woman said. "Lizette Moon. I am the head director."

Ydana remained silent as Mrs. Moon led her to the dining room and pointed to each of the girls seated at the table.

"That is Charity, Meryn, Aurelia, Sissy," she pointed to the girls Ydana recognized as Charity's friends from her brief sighting the night before, "Neda, Sakineh," she pointed to two Hashemi girls who briefly eyed Ydana before turning back to each other to continue the conversation.

"Caprice, Vianne," she pointed to two other Grusrecian girls who were also wrapped up in conversation and barely spared Ydana a glance, "and Misty."

Misty, the manticore girl from the hallway the previous night, picked at her food without looking up. Ydana could tell that she was Grusrecian rather than Hashemi, and wondered how long she had been in Hashem before she was chosen by a manticore, and if she had transformed yet.

"Girls," Mrs. Moon said more loudly, in a voice that made each girl look up, save Misty. "This is Ydana. She will be staying with us. I expect you all to be kind to her."

Charity and her three friends laughed to themselves, but grew silent as Mrs. Moon eyed them.

Misty had two empty seats between her and Charity's friends, and another empty seat between her and the two Hashemi girls. Seeing no other empty seats, Ydana took the seat between Misty and the two Hashemi girls, who gave her a strange look.

"Hello," Ydana greeted them.

"Hello," Sakineh said before turning back to Neda.

With a sigh, Ydana turned her gaze to the plate that was placed in front of her. Bread, cheese, and vegetables. The only thing that made this meal different from what her mother fed her at home was the bread. Instead of the flat bread that Ydana was used to seeing, this bread was thick and starchy.

Thankful that she had hunted the night before, even if it was only meager prey, Ydana began picking at her food, eating a few bites of it while mostly just staring at her plate, deep in thought.

"What are lunch and dinner like?" she mustered the courage to address Misty.

Still picking at her food, Misty remained silent for so long that Ydana began to doubt she would say anything at all.

"More of the same, mostly," Misty finally whispered.

"How do you cope with the same old drab vegetables?" Ydana whispered back.

"I'd like to just eat my food, if you don't mind," Misty's tone held a note of finality.

Staring back at her plate, Ydana closed her eyes. She felt the pressure of tears behind her eyes, but she held them back. Charity's laughter from across the table strengthened Ydana's will to hold her tears back, and she began eating the food on her plate, if only to have something to distract herself with.

Once breakfast time was finished, the girls separated according to age group, and went to their classes. Ydana surmised that Neda, Vianne and Caprice were all seventeen, for they all left together in the same direction. Sakineh, Sissy and Aurelia, who Ydana guessed were a year or two younger than her, departed together in a different direction. As Charity, Meryn and Misty left together, Ydana wondered what she was supposed to do.

"You're to go with them," Mrs. Moon said.

Ydana reluctantly stood up from the table and followed Misty, Charity and Meryn upstairs. Charity stole a glance behind her at Ydana and Misty, and rolled her eyes.

"As if it weren't bad enough that we had one manticore in our class," she turned back towards Meryn, "now we have two."

"It's as if they let anyone in these days just to keep the school from closing," Meryn giggled. "But who knows, perhaps those two will embrace their manticore nature and fly off into the woods."

"I doubt that," Charity laughed. "They would be outcasts. I'm willing to bet that whatever manticores stung them regretted it. That's why they never came for them."

Ydana kept her face expressionless, but her fists were clenched at her sides. Did Val regret stinging her? She had seemed perfectly fine with Ydana saying she was not interested in any sort of relationship. Perhaps it was as Charity said, and Ydana was not good enough. If that were the case, it was just as well that she never saw Val again. After all, she had mentioned having stung others, so Ydana imagined that she had someone else somewhere.

Ydana spent the rest of the morning studying grammar, and the afternoon studying mathematics. The only good thing about her time in class was the fact that Miss Wickham was her teacher, and seemed understanding of what a difficult time Ydana was having with her classmates.

In the break between grammar and mathematics, all ten students ate lunch. This was not a meal eaten at the table unless the girls wanted to sit there (which only Charity's group of friends did). Ydana elected to eat her meal outside. She saw Sakineh, Neda, Vianne and Caprice gathered together on the other side of the field and felt somewhat foolish eating alone, but there was no sign of Misty.

Once mathematics was over, Charity and Meryn left the classroom, but Misty stayed in her seat. Ydana stood to leave, but Miss Wickham bade her sit down again.

"This is where you will have your extra lessons," she said.

"Extra lessons?" Ydana had not heard anything about extra lessons, but seeing as Misty had not left her seat, she suspected that it had something to do with being a manticore.

"Manners and the like," Miss Wickham clarified. "Mrs. Moon will be here once she dismisses the older girls. I have to teach music now."

Once Miss Wickham was gone, Ydana turned to Misty.

"Please don't tell me this is some nonsense about controlling our manticore nature."

Misty only stared at the math problems in her book.

"Why are you always avoiding me?" Ydana stood in front of Misty. "Wouldn't you rather we stick together?"

Misty looked up. "You're nothing like me. I've been here since I was twelve while I imagine you at least have a family. Don't tell me your experience as a manticore is the same as mine."

"I thought they only took students 14 and above."

"Well, they made an exception for me. My father and stepmother sent me here and quickly forgot all about me. During my first week, there were so many pranks pulled on me and so many insults hurled my way that I stayed as inconspicuous as possible so that the older girls would have no reason to bother me. Every time my tormentors came of age and left the school, new ones took their place. As long as I give them no reason to shave off all of my hair, put glue in between the pages of my schoolbooks, or leave dead rodents in my bed, they don't. But if I fight back, they will start doing those things again."

Ydana was taken aback. How could anyone be so horrible as to pull those pranks? And on a girl as young as twelve, no less.

"So don't try to be nice to me," Misty continued. "Don't defend me or help me. It's every manticore for herself around here."

"If you don't want to talk to me, fine," Ydana sat down in her seat and crossed her arms, not looking at Misty. "But if you don't have family or any reason to stay here, why do you? Why don't you just fly away?"

"Because a manticore doesn't transform until they meet the one who chose them, or so I hear."

"You haven't met another manticore?" Ydana looked back at Misty.

"Have you?" Misty was surprised.

As soon as Ydana opened her mouth to answer, the door opened, and Mrs. Moon walked in.

"I apologize for my tardiness, girls, but I had a few things to gather," she set a tea kettle down onto the table.

A young woman, who Mrs. Moon briefly introduced as Miss Faye Adams, the teacher of the younger girls, came in after her, carrying a box. Once Miss Adams set the box onto the table, she left, closing the door behind her.

"Today, we will begin by practicing how to behave at a tea party," Mrs. Moon removed three tea cups from the box.

The next hour was filled with Ydana and Misty being scolded if they slurped their tea, no matter how hot it was, being told how to hold their cups, and being made to pause for a certain length of time between sips. Ydana had never been so bored in her life. Her tea was cold by the time she finished one cup.

The tea lesson complete, the girls then had to choose from a list of phrases which were acceptable and which ones were considered impolite, before finally moving on to a discussion of how to avert one's gaze from prey when it wanders past in situations where chasing it would be socially unacceptable.

When Ydana and Misty were finally dismissed, Ydana's head ached terribly. Wandering around the upper floor on the way to her room, she heard beautiful music coming from one of the rooms. Peeking through the door, she saw an empty room laden with nothing but paintings and mirrors, and Miss Wickham, Sissy, and Caprice sat to one side, so focused that they did not notice Ydana.

In the center of the room sat Charity, playing the strings of a harp. Ydana's jaw dropped. She had never expected such beautiful music to come from such an obnoxious person. She lost herself so deeply that it wasn't until the music stopped and the other girls in the room clapped, that Ydana remembered where she was. As Miss Wickham was deciding which girl should perform next, Ydana continued down the hall.

As she left the music room behind, she heard violin and flute music coming from just ahead of her. Peeking into the next room, she saw a smaller music room, in which Vianne and Neda played violins, while Sakineh accompanied them on a flute. Miss Adams looked on, sitting beside Aurelia and Meryn, who each held their own flutes.

Once again, Ydana stood, transfixed, until the girls stopped playing and were dismissed.

After dinner, which mercifully contained some meat, Ydana pulled Miss Wickham aside as the other girls were leaving the table.

"I want to learn to play the harp. Or the violin, or the flute, or do some other activity that isn't extra etiquette to combat my manticore nature. It's not helpful, and I don't find it fair, either."

"While I agree that it isn't fair," Miss Wickham led Ydana outside, "not a lot can be done, I'm afraid."

At Ydana's dismayed expression, Miss Wickham looked abashed.

"Don't worry, child, it's not that I won't at least see what I can do. I just happen to know that Mrs. Moon will demand that you exhibit no manticore tendencies at all before she would even think about releasing you from etiquette lessons. And that means no looking hungrily at a rabbit that passes by, none of that talking back I hear you doing at Charity during class, not even a growl of your stomach if you go too long without raw meat. And I know how difficult that is to control, because Misty has spent the past four years here trying to control those same aspects of herself that make her a manticore, and she still salivates every time she even sees a mouse."

Ydana knew perfectly well how impossible a task that was. After all, she had hunted a rabbit in Lord Warrington's garden with no care for the blood she spilled onto her dress.

"The way you try to repress Misty's manticore nature is only making it worse. And that's what will happen to me if I'm not free to be what I am," Ydana nearly growled as she spoke. "Just like the way my mother forbade me any meat until the day came when I hunted a rabbit in the middle of a party. Why can't we just eat meat when we want it so that our hunger won't be so obvious?"

"I'm not saying I disagree with you," Miss Wickham placed a hand on Ydana's shoulder. "I'm only saying that Mrs. Moon would never allow it. If you want me to ask her, I will, but I'm sure you would rather I not let her know that you're struggling with this, or that the etiquette classes are not enough, because that's precisely how she will see it."

As soon as night fell, Ydana flew from her window in search of prey. In the air, she was tempted to keep flying all the way until she reached home, but knew that would hardly be safe if the manticore hunters knew where she lived. It would be quite some time before her family returned home in any case, and Ydana would be far less safe at home by herself.

Instead, she ate a few mice and pigeons in the woods a short distance away. By the time she flew back to her room at the Academy, she realized that she had not seen the manticore she had caught a glimpse of the previous evening. If it had truly been a manticore, though Ydana had little idea what else it could have been.

She had lost any hope that it had been Val, for the very idea that she would have traveled all this way just to see her was preposterous. She thought it more likely that the manticore she had seen was the one who had stung Misty, come back for her.

No sooner had Ydana climbed into bed, than a knock sounded at the door. With a sigh, she got out of bed and opened the door. To her surprise, she found Misty, who hastily slipped past her and into the room, with a nervous glance at the room across the hall where Charity and her friends were talking.

"What's wrong?" Ydana closed the door.

"I didn't want those girls to see me," Misty stood awkwardly in the middle of the room. "I want to know…how is it that you've met another manticore and fully turned? I would have thought…"

"That I'd have flown away by now? Yes, I did meet the manticore who stung me, but it's…not like that. She isn't interested in me in the least."

"Is that possible?" Misty scratched her head. "I thought the fact that you can survive their sting means it's impossible not to fall in love."

"It would appear that it also means you're just good friends," Ydana hoped she was keeping the dismay from her voice. She didn't want this girl she barely knew thinking she was sad about Val, even if that was the truth. "I'm thinking that must also mean that you can transform without having met the manticore who stung you."

A sad look came into Misty's eyes.

"I've tried that. I've been trying since I first came here."

Ydana thought back to the first time she had transformed into a full manticore. She had indeed met Val, and seen her transform, but that alone had not prompted her to. It had been only after Val had left, that the party guests in the garden had chased her off, that she had transformed. She hoped that it would not take a similar situation for Misty to transform.

"Try to transform along with me," Ydana said before changing into a manticore as Misty covered her mouth with her hand, her eyes wide.

Hardly able to move in the small room, Ydana kept her wings close to her sides. One twitch of her tail knocked a hairbrush from her dresser, and she glanced over her shoulder towards the door to make sure no one had heard. Charity's friends' laughter from across the hall still sounded, and Ydana exhaled, relieved.

"Could…could you do that again?" Misty's voice was small.

Ydana sank to the ground in her human form, her hands and feet on the ground. Wiping the dirt from her hands, she stood up.

"Are you ready?" Ydana waited for Misty to nod before taking her manticore form once more.

This time, Misty was less surprised, though not by much, as she kept her eyes locked on Ydana and concentrated.

A moment passed, and Misty still didn't transform.

"Lamps out, ladies!" Miss Wickham's voice called from down the hall, followed by several groans from Charity and her friends.

"I'm hopeless," Misty said.

"We can figure this out," Ydana said, human once more. "There has to be a way for you to transform. I just know it."

A knock sounded at the door, startling both girls into silence. The door opened, and Miss Wickham peeked into the room.

"I'm glad you two are getting along, but it's time for bed."

Ydanna nodded at Miss Wickham, as Misty hurried out the door without so much as a goodbye. Once Misty and Miss Wickham had gone, and the buzz of conversation in the room across the hall resumed, Ydana sat by the window and looked at the field below.

Before long, a figure walked past, hidden in shadow. It was so dark out that most people wouldn't have spotted the person, but a manticore's eyes were better than most. When the figure looked up in Ydana's direction, their eyes reflected the light.

## CHAPTER SIX

Another week went by with no sign of the manticore she had seen, Val or otherwise. Meal times were just as awkward, Misty had spoken very little to Ydana since the night she had tried to transform, and Charity and her friends were no less unfriendly.

Etiquette lessons had moved on from tea parties to more difficult tasks. For the past few days, Mrs. Moon had brought mice and rabbits to class, and letting them loose around the room to teach Ydana and Misty control over their manticore urges. They had both been unable to resist nearly every time, and earned no supper as a result. Ydana hunted at night so that she would not starve, but felt terrible for Misty, who could not. Even if Misty would accept help, sneaking a dead bird or mouse to her was too difficult to do without being seen.

On Ydana's ninth day at the Academy, she had been sent to her room without supper yet again. Despite the early hour, she stared out the window, looking for the manticore she had seen. She had hoped it was Val, which made her feel foolish all over again. But if a manticore had come for Misty, surely, they would have shown themselves already.

The only people in the field below were Charity and her fiancée, who Ydana had not known existed until he stopped by to visit. Ydana watched Charity realize whose window she was standing under, and usher her fiancée away from there.

In the bushes just beyond the couple, a pair of eyes gleamed in the light. Only it was not the mysterious manticore from before, but Misty, her eyes trained on something near Charity's feet. Ydana looked closer and saw a mouse, which must have been what was of interest to Misty.

To Ydana's horror, Misty pounced from the bushes, to land in front of Charity and devour the mouse, her face covered in blood. Charity's screams alerted Miss Wickham, Miss Adams and Mrs. Moon, who were followed by some of the girls.

"Take that thing away!" Charity's fiancée was holding her as she hid her face in his jacket.

As Misty ran across the field, she slowly changed until she was running on all fours, a full manticore. But before she made it the whole way across, Charity's fiancée shoved her aside and took something from the inside of his coat. From her view from the window, Ydana could not see what it was he threw at Misty, but the manticore crumpled to the ground, human once more, with the half-eaten mouse still in her mouth.

Getting up, Ydana rushed from the room, not bothering to close the door behind her. When she came downstairs and ran out to the yard, she was relieved to at least find that Miss Adams and Miss Wickham were helping Charity's fiancée tie ropes around Misty's feet. Seeing as this meant that Misty was still alive, Ydana breathed a sigh of relief.

"What's going to happen to her?" her voice sounded smaller than she would have liked.

Looking surprised to find Ydana standing there, Miss Wickham came to stand beside her, as Charity's fiancée looked disgusted to see another manticore.

"I'm not supposed to be telling you this, but it's most likely she will be taken to a madhouse," Miss Wickham whispered. "Not just because she is a manticore, but also because her parents have failed to pay her tuition this year. We have written them again and again with no reply. Please don't tell Mrs. Moon I said so."

"If her parents have stopped paying, can't you just let her be free? Her life is her own business if she won't be here anymore and has no family," Ydana thought she would cry. "What's wrong with letting her fly away?"

"Thank you so much, Lyle, for your quick thinking," Mrs. Moon was congratulating Charity's fiancée.

Ydana spun around to see them, but Miss Wickham stepped in front of her. It was only then that she realized that Mrs. Moon had not yet noticed Ydana standing next to Miss Wickham in the dark. She kept her head down to prevent any chance of her eyes reflecting the light and drawing attention to her.

"It's no problem," Lyle replied. "It's what they train us for, after all. We can't afford to let a manticore get the best of us. I will send word to my associates who can deal with her in a more appropriate manner."

A shiver went up Ydana's spine at the way Lyle spoke so calmly about 'dealing with' Misty. She clenched her fists, wishing she could transform right then and there without meeting the same fate as Misty. Even if she caught him by surprise, she would be out cold if he had even a moment to draw his weapon.

"We have somewhere we can keep her until they arrive," Mrs. Moon said.

"Lead the way," Lyle went to Misty and hoisted her cruelly over his shoulder.

"How can you even touch her?" Charity called from a few feet away.

"Necessity, my darling," Lyle called back as he made his way to the doors of the Academy.

There was nothing Ydana could do to hide before Lyle walked past her, and she did not need to look up to see that he had spotted her.

"That's another one behind you, miss," he said to Miss Wickham. "My associates can do something about her, too."

"She hasn't turned, and hopefully won't," Miss Wickham placed her hands on her hips. "Keep walking and leave my student alone."

"Just consider yourself warned," Lyle called over his shoulder as he continued walking. "Manticores are dangerous, and they can only be killed one way, so you won't stand a chance against one."

So that was why he hadn't killed Misty. It wasn't because he didn't want to, or because she was needed alive, but because he had to call in someone else to do the deed. As soon as Lyle and Mrs. Moon were gone, Ydana realized that she was shaking. She had half a mind to simply take off through the bushes and run away someplace else, but she knew she didn't stand a chance. Manticore hunters were no longer simply a scary story, but a very real danger.

That night, when everyone had finally gone to bed, Ydana searched all around the mansion for Misty, moving slowly so as not to make any noise as she searched. It was only as daylight was breaking that she found the door that led to the basement. When she heard the sounds of the kitchen staff preparing the morning meal, she knew that there was not much time.

Closing the basement door behind her lest she be discovered, she descended the stairs.

"Misty?" she whispered.

A muffled response answered her.

Following the sound, Ydana ran past the shelves to a corner of the basement. Bound and gagged, Misty looked up.

"I'm so glad you're alright," Ydana pulled the gag off of Misty and began untying the ropes around her wrists. "We have to get out of here. Can you transform again?"

"Not with these ropes," Misty shook her hands free of the ropes as if they were something disgusting. "And not just because of the ropes. They did something to keep me from transforming, I'm sure of it. I can try again, but I'm not sure if it will work."

"How were you able to transform?" Ydana picked at the ropes that bound Misty's ankles. "Did you meet another manticore?"

"No, I hadn't transformed before, until last night," Misty stood up once she was free of the ropes. "It's not fair of them to starve us."

"I know," Ydana whispered. "And I overheard them last night, saying that your parents have stopped paying your tuition. Wherever they're sending you is nowhere good. We have to leave."

A dismayed look in her eyes, Misty nodded and followed Ydana to the door.

"If we're going to remove her without waking the rest of the girls," came a voice from outside of the basement that Ydana recognized as Mrs. Moon's, "you will likely have to sedate her again."

Behind Ydana, Misty froze.

"She's in here, gentlemen," Mrs. Moon's voice sounded from outside of the basement door.

Shoving Ydana behind her, Misty transformed. As if it weren't enough that Ydana was out of the way, Misty shoved her down the stairs with her tail, where she tripped and stumbled around the corner.

Above Ydana came the sound of the door opening, followed by Misty's roar that shook the basement. When Ydana peered around the corner, daylight was filtering inside of the basement through the open door, and Misty and her aggressors were all gone.

Running up the stairs and out to the field, she saw Misty flying away, dodging what was shot at her. Ydana then understood why Misty had shoved her out of the way. To leave with Misty now would be making a dangerous getaway, and at the very least, no one here seemed to know that Ydana had turned. Ydana could stay at the Academy until her family passed back through in a week, and explain to them what had happened. Surely her family would not insist she stay at a boarding school that manticore hunters had just come to.

Not daring to look around the corner at the manticore hunters, lest they see her, Ydana kept her eye on Misty. When the weapons being fired grew fewer and farther between, Ydana breathed a sigh of relief. But no sooner had she done so, than two small winged contraptions flew through the air after Misty. They were not very fast, and each one held perhaps two people, but Ydana was sure they had weapons aboard.

Once Misty and her pursuers had disappeared into the morning fog, Ydana heard the other manticore hunters in the field pack up and leave to go after them.

At breakfast, all anyone could talk about was what had happened to Misty the night before.

"I was so disgusted," Charity whined. "The last thing anyone needs is someone jumping in front of you eating a mouse!"

"Do not worry, girls," Mrs. Moon said. "She has been taken care of."

"Was she caught, and sent to a madhouse?" Aurelia asked.

"Precisely," Mrs. Moon said. "She has been taken somewhere where she will be taken care of."

Ydana could hardly eat her food. Either Mrs. Moon was lying to put the girls at ease, or Misty had indeed been caught. Either way, Ydana felt uneasy. She didn't want to listen to the rest of the conversation, but realized that she had to, just in case she heard any pertinent information.

"I'm so glad she's gone," Meryn wrinkled her nose. "This will make our time here so much more enjoyable."

"You're right, things will be much better without her in the way," Charity said.

Around the table, Neda, Sakineh, Caprice and Vianne all looked at each other. Ydana guessed that they were thinking the same thing she was, that with Misty absent, Charity's group of friends would simply pick on someone else. If it wasn't Ydana, it could easily be any of them. The older girls had less of a chance of being picked on, but Sakineh was both Hashemi and the youngest at the academy.

It was then that Ydana realized that she did not know what lengths the other girls would go to to make sure that Ydana, and not one of them, was Charity's next victim. She hoped that it would not be a lot of lengths, seeing as they were all friends, making Ydana, the loner among them, the obvious target by default.

"But if she turned, doesn't that mean that the manticore who chose her is nearby?" Sissy asked.

"Never fear, girls," Mrs. Moon said. "He has likely gone by now, and we will have people stopping by to check every night for the time being, in case he has not."

Ydana choked on her water. There would be no more hunting at night for her, lest she be seen by a manticore hunter. And now that she knew that the manticore she had seen walking around at night was not there for Misty, there was every chance he, or perhaps she, was still around. She had to find a way to warn the manticore.

"We should still watch out," Meryn said. "There could be another manticore coming for *her* any time."

Surprised, Ydana inhaled sharply when Meryn pointed a fork at her.

"No one is coming for me, remember?" Ydana glared at Meryn. "You said yourself that I'm too plain. That the manticore who stung me probably regretted doing so. Therefore, I would appreciate it if you stopped talking about me as if I'm not right here."

"That's enough, Ydana!" Mrs. Moon said sharply.

"So she admits she's too plain," Charity whispered to Meryn.

"There will be no more harsh words at the table, girls," Mrs. Moon scolded.

Groans of dismay came from Charity and her friends, while the other girls sighed in relief. Ydana simply stared into her uneaten food.

In class, Ydana stayed out of Charity and Meryn's way as much as possible, trying to make them forget that she was even there now that it was only the three of them without Misty. Ydana didn't raise her hand to answer a question or even look up from her books for fear of Miss Wickham calling on her. It was then that she truly realized how terrible it must have been for Misty to be the only manticore at the school for as long as she was.

Thankfully, Miss Wickham appeared to be on Ydana's side, and dispelled any rude comments that came Ydana's way from the other girls. Once class was over, Miss Wickham waited until Meryn and Charity had left before leaving the room, to make sure that they didn't have a chance to pick on Ydana.

Ydana already knew that that was all the help she would get from Miss Wickham, who did not offer any comfort or suggestions once the other girls had gone. Instead, she stayed in the room, silent, as if not knowing what one could possibly say that would make Ydana's situation any better.

"What are you still doing here, Miss Wickham? Don't you have a music class to teach?" Mrs. Moon came in through the door, holding a cage that contained three rabbits. The rabbits immediately began to shake as soon as they saw Ydana. Ydana had to look out through the window so that neither of the teachers would see her salivating.

When Miss Wickham hesitated, Ydana thought for one moment that perhaps her teacher was about to suggest that Ydana attend music class instead of etiquette, or that she at least be allowed supper.

But Miss Wickham simply grumbled an "Of course, Mrs. Moon," and left the room.

A.R. Hellbender

"Now that our longest-standing student has, regrettably, left us," Mrs. Moon placed the cage on the floor, "it is all the more crucial that you avoid becoming a full manticore."

## CHAPTER SEVEN

Ydana wanted to laugh. She had figured since coming to the Academy that no one knew she had already turned, but was not sure if her parents had told them she hadn't or if it has simply been assumed. If it was merely Mrs. Moon's assumption, it was a stupid one.

"Therefore," Mrs. Moon continued, "it is crucial that you suppress your manticore nature as much as possible."

"Mrs. Moon," Ydana raised her hand.

"I will do the speaking here," Mrs. Moon scowled at her. "If you are going to be as human as the rest of us, you must control yourself and not interrupt me."

"But you were starving us with these lessons," Ydana protested. "That's why Misty turned!"

"Nonsense," Mrs. Moon unlatched the cage door and banged on it until the three rabbits that were cowering against the back wall of it finally jumped out. "If you chase even one of those rabbits, you will be sent to your room with no supper."

Ydana had only even remotely survived the past few of these lessons better than Misty had because she was able to hunt at night. Having not hunted the previous night due to Misty's being caught, she had gone with no meat for two whole days. How would she ever survive now?

Plugging her nose, she breathed through her mouth so that less of the scent of delicious rabbit would reach her. But then it occurred to her that if she didn't eat one of these rabbits, she would go hungry. On all fours before she realized it, she lunged at the nearest rabbit, tearing into it with her teeth. It was only the barest of human instinct left that allowed her to keep from turning into a manticore right then and there.

Behind her, Mrs. Moon's screams and scoldings sounded far away. Knowing that Mrs. Moon would hardly dare to interrupt her eating, Ydana tore the meat off of the carcass until none was left.

With blood all over her face and down the front of her gown, Ydana was sure she looked fearsome. Turning towards Mrs. Moon, she stared hard at the shocked old woman.

"If you continue to starve me," Ydana said in the most fearsome voice she could muster, "this is what you will get. If I don't eat rabbits, I'm sure to start eating people eventually. Is that what you want?"

"Go straight to your room this instant, young lady," Mrs. Moon recovered her composure. "You have lost the privilege of lessons and meals with the other girls. You will have to stay in your room, with your meals brought to you."

"Just make sure they're meat," Ydana coolly walked past Mrs. Moon and exited the room.

The next day, Ydana was given class assignments to do independently and did not go to class. She did not even see who brought her meals to her room, as whoever it was simply knocked and left the food by the door. Thankfully, her meals did include some meat, though it was still mostly salad and bread. They clearly thought she was being punished, but she found this far preferable to the company of the other girls.

Towards the end of the day, another knock sounded at her door. Puzzled because it was not meal time, Ydana opened the door to find Miss Wickham.

"Your mother has come to visit," she said.

"My mother?" Ydana was not sure why her mother had come alone, and before their visit with Victor's fiancée was due to be complete, as they had planned for it to be a three-week stay. But she was, nevertheless, glad to have someone to tell about her awful time at the Academy. Hopefully, she could ask her mother to let her come home.

Confused, she followed Miss Wickham downstairs to the sitting room that was reserved for visits from family and the like. There sat Lady Ylaine, next to a Grusrecian gentleman Ydana did not recognize. He looked older than Ydana by at least five years, and the expression on his face was serious. Ydana knew that whoever this stranger was, this was hardly the time to let her mother know that she wished to come home.

"Hello, mother," Ydana stood awkwardly in the center of the room.

"Do sit down, Ydana," her mother said in her usual, cold voice. "This is Diederick Miros, a cousin of Lady Elvira. Lord Miros, this is my daughter, Ydana."

"It's nice to…meet you," Ydana stammered when Lord Miros said nothing.

"A bit plain, is she not?" Lord Miros frowned. "And you neglected to mention that she was a manticore."

"I was hoping that it would not matter," Lady Ylaine offered. "Perhaps if she does not join the manticores, some of her humanity will…return."

Ydana did not like where this conversation was going, and fidgeted in her chair.

"Ydana," her mother addressed her, "Lord Miros is here to make an offer of marriage. He can provide a home for you in Grusrecia where you will be safe. And the wedding would not take place until next year, when you are old enough."

"But I don't want to go to Grusrecia," Ydana protested.

"I'm going to speak with your teachers while you two take a walk in the garden," Lady Ylaine said as if Ydana had not spoken.

When her mother stood up to join Mrs. Moon and Miss Wickham, who had entered the sitting room, Ydana awkwardly left the room and went to the garden, followed by Lord Miros.

"I'm sure you're very nice," Ydana began as they ventured into the garden, "but I can't imagine I'm the one for you."

"I'm certain you're not," Lord Miros continued to frown, "but I must marry someone in order to inherit, and it hardly matters who."

"But would you not want someone…human?" Ydana could think of nothing to do but continue walking further into the garden. "After all, I've already turned."

If Lord Miros was surprised at this, he did not show it. If he thought she was lying about having already turned, Ydana could hardly prove it without someone else seeing.

"It's always the plain women who are ungrateful for every offer that comes their way," he said once they reached the edge of the garden, where the wooded area began.

"Plain?" Ydana frowned. "Ungrateful? I'm simply not interested in being married, and even less so to someone who insults me!"

"You will not speak to me in such a manner!" Lord Miros' sullen but calm demeanor melted away to reveal a harsh tone and an even deeper frown. "Next year when we are to be married, you will have realized by then how little else there is for you in this world, that I truly am the best option you will ever receive. If you do not understand this by that time, I will *make* you understand!"

"I would like to see you try!"

Without any warning, he slapped her. Putting a hand to her stinging cheek, Ydana turned to face him.

"Now you've lost *any* chance of marrying me, against my will or no," Ydana turned back to the Academy. "My mother would never marry me off to someone who hits me, and my father even less so!"

"They will never believe you," he grasped her by the arm. "It's your word against mine, and if you think yours is the one your mother will believe, you are sorely mistaken."

"Let go of me!" Ydana tried to pry his fingers off of her arm, to no avail.

"You *will* listen to me, or I'll—"

Before he could finish his sentence, a new figure sprung from the woods. Before Ydana even registered that Val was standing in front of her, she came up behind Lord Miros and bit him in the side of the neck. Even in human form, Val's teeth bit deeply enough to draw blood.

Ydana stared, wide-eyed, as Lord Miros put a hand to his neck and screamed.

"Go," she whispered, locking eyes with Val and then darting a glance back towards the building.

Seeming to understand what she meant, Val disappeared back into the bushes. As all three teachers and Ydana's mother made their way across the garden, Lord Miros crumpled to his knees.

"Quickly, come with me," Miss Adams helped him up and began leading him back towards the building.

"It's her fault," Lord Miros pointed to Ydana. "That ungrateful trollop has lost her chance!"

"Ydana, what have you done?" Lady Ylaine fixed her gaze on Ydana.

Ydana could only stare, eyes wide. She hardly wanted to give the manticore hunters cause to come back and take her, but she could hardly let anyone know that Val was nearby.

"Take her to her room," Mrs. Moon shouted at Miss Wickham. "And lock the door."

Leaving Mrs. Moon and Lady Ylaine in the garden, Ydana and Miss Wickham made their way inside. Without speaking, Miss Wickham led Ydana up the stairs to her room, shutting the door behind her.

Ydana heard the lock click into place.

## CHAPTER EIGHT

Wasting no time, Ydana packed most of her books and a change of clothing into a pillowcase. The books would be heavy enough for her to use the pillowcase as a weapon if need be. That done, she changed into the most comfortable dress she had, that wasn't too tight at the shoulders or elbows.

She knew that the one advantage she had was that no one at the Academy knew that she had already turned. If she took them by surprise, she could get away before anyone knew.

Opening the window, she turned into a manticore and, grasping the pillowcase in her mouth, jumped from the ledge. Once she was clear of the window and had enough room to spread her wings, she soared upwards. Hearing shouts from below, she turned her head to see that a group of men had arrived, who she guessed were manticore hunters. Eager to leave the scene before they could send their airbound contraptions after her, she flapped her wings faster.

Within moments, she heard a mechanical sound behind her. Without looking back, she dipped down and fell back, letting the flying machine continue ahead of her. Rising up behind it, she brought the pillowcase filled with books down onto the machine's fragile wing, hoping that the weight of the books wouldn't tear the pillowcase. Swooping ahead of the flying machine once more, she turned back to see it struggle to remain air bound.

It was then that she heard a familiar roar that almost sounded like her name. Following the sound, she soon saw a manticore's silhouette in the fog not far ahead. She did not know how long she flew beside Val, but it was well past dark by the time her companion nodded towards a floating island nearby.

Her tired wings aching, Ydana dove towards the island in the sky. Crashing through the trees, she let herself drop to the ground and land on all fours before laying down in her human form, still clutching the pillowcase. It took her a moment to realize that her dress had been torn in her hasty transformation, leaving her mostly in rags that barely covered her. But she was far too tired to care. Beside her, Val took her human form and lay beside her. Looking up through the tops of the trees, Ydana could just barely see the stars, and was comforted knowing that any manticore hunters flying their flimsy two-person flyers overhead would not see them.

"I'm so sorry I got you in trouble like that," Val propped herself up on one arm to look down at Ydana. "When I saw him hurting you, I had to do something. Listening to that odious man insult you was horrible enough."

"It's alright," Ydana smiled. "I'm glad you stepped in. It's thanks to you that the situation became urgent enough for me to escape. I would still be there, too afraid to fly away, were it not for you."

"No. I eventually would have been able to get you out."

"You were trying to help me all along?" Ydana was surprised. "How long were you near there? I thought you had forgotten all about me."

Val's roguish grin lit up her face. "Forget you? Never! I knew you would eventually regret leaving for boarding school, and I fully intended to keep returning to you until you would go with me."

"Thank you, Val. I'm glad you came for me."

"No need to thank me," Val lay down beside Ydana and looked up through the trees.

"Where are we going to go?" Ydana said after a pause. "I can hardly go home now, or else I'll just be sent somewhere else. All of those manticore hunters saw me transform. They know who I am. My home is the first place they'll look for me."

"Don't worry. I have a plan," Val drew Ydana close. It was hard not to fall asleep when she listened to her heartbeat.

After a few hours of sleep, Ydana and Val woke up and continued flying while it was still dark. Ydana didn't know how long they flew, but dawn was finally breaking when Ydana spotted the biggest floating island she had ever seen, surrounded by dozens of smaller islands. She wondered how it was that an island in the sky bigger than the ones she had seen before had never been seen by humans.

As she flew closer, she realized that there were black forms in the sky around the island. They had to be manticores! Beside her, Val let loose a loud roar. From the island came several roars in response. The closer she and Val flew, the more details she was able to notice on the surface of the island. Instead of just trees and clearings, there were entire stone buildings, and even a massive boulder that dwarfed everything around it, on which a group of manticores were resting.

Landing on the ground beside Val, Ydana looked around her, stepping closer to Val at the sight of a group of manticores that were flying towards them. The manticores landed, and Ydana saw that they had the same half-human form that Val had shown her the second time they had met, that had made her look like a lion centaur. Like Val, they all had the dark hair tinged with red that was characteristic of a manticore, as well as the facial features characteristic of Hashemi. Ydana supposed that not many Grusrecians were chosen to be manticores like Misty was.

Taking her human form, Val stepped up to the other manticores.

"If we could take the normal human form, that would be best for Ydana," she looked up at them.

Once the other manticores took their fully human forms, the woman in front embraced Val. She looked young, and Ydana felt a surge of jealousy as she took her own human form, feeling stupid as she clutched the heavy book-filled pillowcase she had brought from the Academy.

This manticore girl was pretty, with large eyes and perfect curls that stuck out in every direction. The garment she wore as a shirt was cropped at her waist and showed off her thin figure. The more Ydana looked at her, the more jealous she felt. Any inkling of hope she had that Val was romantically interested in her was rapidly dwindling, for she did not even compare when there were manticores who looked like this girl. If Val even preferred girls, surely Ydana couldn't compare.

One by one, each manticore present greeted Val, embracing her, as Ydana hung back. Val did not try to introduce her to anyone, perhaps sensing that she was still overwhelmed. Soon, the rest of the group took their manticore forms again and flew away, except for the pretty girl, who remained in human form.

"Is this my replacement?" she stepped past Val towards Ydana.

"This is *Ydana*," Val said as if correcting her. "She's not interested in me that way, so don't be rude."

The manticore girl looked at Ydana and raised an eyebrow, then back at Val.

"Did she tell you that? She's not telling the truth."

"*She* is right here," Ydana was tired of people talking about her as if she weren't there, and she was not about to let someone else do the same, especially when it was her feelings for Val, or lack thereof, they were talking about.

"So you do speak!" the girl turned back towards her, pleasantly surprised. "I'm Tara."

"Ydana," Ydana shook Tara's outstretched hand.

"She's so nervous, Val," Tara said. "Didn't you prepare her for this at all?"

"Regrettably, no," Val sighed. "We had to make a quick getaway to avoid some manticore hunters."

"You're joking!" Tara looked, wide-eyed, at Ydana. Evidently Tara's own transformation had not been quite as eventful. "We should take her to the boulder!"

A few moments later, Ydana was following Val and Tara through the air, to land on the large boulder that several manticores were resting on. Turning human once more, Ydana looked around her at the view of the landscape in the light from the pink sunrise.

"Wow, it's beautiful!" she sat down as close to the edge of the boulder as she dared go.

"This is the highest spot on the whole island," Val took her human form to sit beside her, Tara on the other side. "You can see nearly everything from here."

Her shoulder touched Val's, and she half expected her to put an arm around her, or try to hold her hand, but she knew, at the same time, that she wouldn't. Once the sun had risen completely, and the buildings were more visible, Val and Tara began pointing things out to Ydana.

"That's where Val lives," Tara pointed to a white stone building mostly hidden behind tall trees. "And further in that direction is the lake, and that's where all of the best hunting is."

"How can there be a lake?" Ydana wondered. "We're in the sky."

"It fills up with rain water and condensation from the clouds," Val explained.

"Where do you live, Tara?" Ydana asked.

"Oh, I'm a…roamer, like many manticores. I sleep under the stars, and I keep my belongings wherever. Or at Val's house," Tara smiled. "Most manticores, even those with actual dwellings, spend most of their time outside, even to sleep. I used to think that was strange when I first arrived here, so I'm sure it's not what you're used to, either."

Noticing how few actual buildings of any kind were around, Ydana began wondering where she would stay. If there were any caves on the island, they would surely be taken up by solitary manticores who would shoo anyone else away. Realizing just how alone she truly was, she felt tears building up behind her eyes and struggled to hold them at bay lest she cry in front of Val and Tara.

"You'll be staying with me for as long as you want to," Val leaned in to whisper in her ear. "I could even build you your own dwelling if you wanted. But sharing mine would be much more fun."

Feeling a blush creep to her face, Ydana didn't know how to respond. Though the thought of living with Val was a good one, she had no idea how she could bear moving out one day once Val stung another human in whom she was actually interested. Part of her hoped that Val would settle for her, but another, more sensible part knew that it was hardly worth it if either of them were only settling. Within the next century, Val was sure to find someone else, though a century still seemed like an incomprehensible amount of time.

"I'd be happy to," Ydana whispered back. "Stay with you, I mean. Just feel free to kick me out if I'm too annoying."

"Hardly," Val finally wrapped an arm around her, before sitting up more to peer down below. "Oh, there's Amin and Misha. I should say hello before they hear from someone else that I'm back and didn't greet them."

"I'll take care of Ydana," Tara moved to sit next to Ydana as soon as Val stood up.

"And I, for my part, will return as quickly as I can," Val looked back down at Ydana once more before taking her half-manticore form and leaping off of the edge of the boulder.

Once Val was gone, Ydana turned to Tara.

"So...were you a human once?" she asked, though she knew the answer, having seen that Tara's wings were feathered like her own, and not batlike the way a natural manticore's were.

"Yes," Tara laughed. "But Val and I were not meant to be. Except as best friends, of course."

"Do you have someone else?" Ydana felt awkward asking, but she was curious.

"Definitely not," Tara smiled. "I rather like being on my own. I may get tired of it in a few hundred years, but not before then."

Trying to laugh along with her, Ydana wished she could be more like Tara. Unsure of what else to say, she stared out over the landscape, looking for something that Tara and Val had not already pointed out to her. Failing that, she looked backwards at the many more manticores who were gathering on the boulder now that the sun had risen.

"She's interested in you; I hope you realize."

Tara's voice nearly made Ydana jump.

"Val, I mean," Tara smiled at her.

"If you think Val has feelings for me, I'm afraid you are sorely mistaken," Ydana hugged her knees to her chest and rested her head on her knees. "If you weren't enough to capture her attention that way, then I'm certainly not."

"I've known her for nearly 50 years, and I can tell. But if you're only interested in her for her title, believe me, I will end you."

"Her title?" Ydana struggled to recall anything Val may have said about such a thing. "What title?"

Tara looked as if she were about to laugh, before covering her mouth in surprise.

"You really *don't* know, do you?"

"Don't know what?" Val appeared before them in her half human form.

Before Tara or Ydana could formulate an answer, several manticores came to stand behind them, towering over Ydana in their half human, half manticore forms.

"Your highness," one of them said, "you're finally back!"

Ydana's jaw dropped, and she stole a glance at Val, who was looking embarrassed. Before she could say anything, Tara grasped her by the hand and pulled her away from the crowd. She wasn't even scared as Tara, in half manticore form, lifted her off of the ground and flew her down from the boulder.

Once Tara set her onto the ground, Ydana flung the pillowcase she was still carrying onto the ground.

"She didn't tell you?" Tara stood before Ydana, fully human once more.

"She did not," she answered. *And now I know for sure that she has no feelings for me*, she thought.

# CHAPTER NINE

Sasha had barely finished eating breakfast when he received a summons from his father. In the library, his father and mother were both waiting for him, and next to them stood a Hashemi woman he did not recognize.

She was about his age, and would have been pretty if her curls weren't done up in such an elaborate style complete with a hair clip that had a sheer purple veil attached to it that all but covered her eyes, and if her purple dress weren't so arrayed in frills. The fact that she even wore a dress made with such expensive dye made Sasha uneasy, as she should hardly have any reason to flaunt her wealth during a private visit such as this.

"Mother, father," Sasha hesitantly greeted his parents before turning to the young lady.

"This is the Podishah's niece, Princess Sahar," his father said before Sasha had a chance to introduce himself. "She has come to ask to be married to you."

Sasha's jaw dropped. The Hashemi custom was for a woman to do the asking, and he realized that her reason for wearing a dress worthy of a significant social gathering was to impress his parents and win their approval. Though the fact that she was a princess should have been enough.

"It's...nice to meet you," Sasha was unsure of what to say when meeting a pretty girl who wanted to marry you.

Instead of replying, she simply smiled. Clearly she had no more of an idea of what to say than he did.

"Before we allow you two to become better acquainted," his mother said, "there is something else to discuss."

Sneaking a glance at Princess Sahar, Sasha realized that she knew better than he did what was coming.

Taking a book from a nearby desk, his mother flipped it open to a specific page and handed it to Sasha.

"What is this?" he said before even looking at the book.

When his mother said nothing, he looked at the top of the page, where the book's title was written above the text.

"Manticores?" he looked up at his parents. "Why…"

"Keep reading," his mother prompted.

Not knowing why, he was being made to read about manticores, of all things, and in front of a guest, he looked down at the page his mother had opened the book to and continued reading.

The chapter was titled 'Manticore Hunting', and went on to describe how the people of centuries ago, both in Hashem and its surrounding kingdoms, began hunting manticores, and why. Most of the Hashemi families did so because children of theirs were stung and turned into manticores, while most of the people who came in from Grusrecia to hunt manticores did so for the monetary rewards.

According to the book, most manticore hunters made their hunting a family business and kept these dealings out of the public eye. Therefore, very few manticore hunters were known by name anymore. It surprised Sasha to know that even the Grusrecian manticore hunters, who he would have thought would love to brag about their accomplishments, kept their hunting expeditions into Hashem a secret, claiming to be gone on business. Part of this was because they were not usually expecting to return successful and were afraid of being laughed at, but they were also afraid of other manticores learning who they were and coming after them.

"What does this have to do with me?" Sasha lifted his gaze from the book. "Or Princess Sahar?"

"Everything," his mother's expression was serious.

"Your mother and I are both descended from manticore hunters," his father said, "and it is time you learned. Princess Sahar, like most of the Hashemi royals, is an accomplished manticore hunter herself and can show you everything you need to know about the weapons used against a manticore. Though the manticores only rarely interfere with humans, you have seen the damage that just one can inflict."

"You both may leave us," his mother sat down at her desk. "Take Princess Sahar out to the garden and show her around."

Princess Sahar turned to leave the library, but Sasha did not move.

"Did Leon truly disappear from boarding school?"

"That is nothing for you to worry about," his mother replied again. "You could never understand the decisions we had to make for Leon."

Sasha wanted to protest, but remembered that Princess Sahar was still in the room, and she hardly cared about what happened to one boy turned manticore long ago. He didn't even know the princess, but it would not do to annoy her. Clenching his fists, he left the room to join her in the hallway.

Fire Consumes Us

"How did you know you wanted to marry me?" he did his best to put on a more cheerful tone as he walked her outside in the direction of the garden. "I was not aware that you knew of my existence."

"I saw you at your father's ball," she placed a hand on the arm he offered to her. "First, when you stood up for your friend, the manticore, and again later when you said something to my father to make him laugh. I guessed that anyone who can make my father laugh must be unique indeed."

He remembered the incident she was describing. Having encountered the Podishah's brother, he was at a loss of what to say and had been so awkward in complimenting a piece of jewelry he did not know the name of, that the man had actually laughed.

What surprised him more was that the princess was complimenting him on having stood up for a manticore, for he hardly would have expected such a thing from someone who had supposedly killed at least one of the creatures.

"You're...glad that I stood up for a manticore?" Sasha asked.

"Of course," Princess Sahar smiled. "I'm not happy that you are friends with a manticore, of course, and I would expect you to end that friendship once we are married, but I appreciate that you stood up for someone lesser than yourself. It's a good quality in a leader."

Sasha wanted to feel happy about receiving such a compliment from a princess, but something bothered him about what she had said.

"I'm sure that's true, but...she was hardly lesser than me. She was your cousin, the daughter of Lord Azra Veshteh."

"Oh, how terrible for him," she looked away. "But...what do you mean 'was'? Did she leave after the ball, when she transformed?"

"Shortly after, yes," Sasha was hardly going to go into everything that had happened with Ydana. He hoped that she had flown away from boarding school by now and was safe. Especially now that he was soon to be engaged, he hoped that Ydana had found happiness with someone of her own kind. Especially if humans more than just hated manticores, but hunted them.

"Have you ever killed a manticore?" Sasha could not help but ask.

"Several," the princess answered, her lips curving upwards into a smile. It unnerved Sasha that he could barely see her eyes and could thusly tell very little of what she was thinking.

"What sorts of weapons do you use?"

"To kill them? No, we learn to fight merely for defense, and for capture. There is only one way to kill a manticore, and it cannot be done in battle."

Sasha had a feeling that he did not want to find out what

## CHAPTER TEN

"What you need is a distraction," Tara led Ydana through the forest.

Both girls were running on all fours, Ydana in manticore form, and Tara still with a human torso so that she could talk.

"You are sure to adjust to being a manticore if I show you around a bit more. Our first stop is where I've been spending most of my time lately," Tara parted the tree branches to reveal a small clearing.

Once in her human form, Tara knelt by the lone pile of objects that sat next to a tree at the edge of the clearing, and sifted through her belongings. Ydana spotted only a bow, arrows, several flasks of water, and a few books, next to a backpack. The rest was a mountain of cloth.

"What sort of clothing did you bring with you?" Tara asked.

Dropping the pillowcase she still carried in her mouth, Ydana turned from manticore to human and untied the knot that held it closed. Turning the pillowcase upside down, she spilled the books and one dress out onto the ground.

"Well, I see where your priorities are," Tara smirked.

"I had no time to pack. This was mostly meant as a weapon in case I had to hit someone with it."

"Smart girl. You can actually trade those for pretty much anything around here, too. We have a library, but it's far from up to date. Very few of us acquire any new books when visiting the mainland, after all."

"Oh, I suppose that's…good to know," Ydana had never thought she would consider trading her books away, but under the circumstances, she was glad to know that they could get her useful items if she needed them.

Tara examined the lone dress that did not look much different from what Ydana already had on, save that it was intact. "This won't help you much. Using the fabric from your dresses to make some more practical clothing would be much more useful. But for now, I can let you have something of mine."

After sifting through the pile of clothing she had, Tara brought out a piece of cloth so small that it didn't even look like a shirt.

"Where are the sleeves?" Ydana could hardly imagine herself wearing anything like what Tara was wearing.

"When you figure out how to leave your upper half human while the bottom half turns into a manticore and keep your clothing intact, I'm sure you don't want to be wearing a dress," Tara held out the meager shirt to her. "You'd just be laughed at. And you'd trip over the hem of your dress, too."

Reluctantly, Ydana took the shirt and a pair of trousers from Tara and, looking over her shoulder to make sure no one else was about, changed out of her dress. She had worn trousers a few times, but wearing such a short shirt that showed her stomach was entirely new to her. Once she was dressed, she self-consciously covered her stomach.

"Try to transform into this form," Tara took on her half manticore form as she spoke.

Taking a deep breath, Ydana transformed, but knew before she even opened her eyes that all she had succeeded in doing was taking full manticore form. Trying again from there, she transformed back into a human.

"It must be too early for me to attempt this sort of thing," Ydana slumped to the ground with a sigh.

"It takes time," Tara knelt beside Ydana, human once more. "I just wanted to see if you could do it now that you were wearing more comfortable clothes, because that helps tremendously. But it's more likely that the first time you take that form will happen when it's really needed."

Ydana began wondering if she should attempt to make her own clothing, out of the dress she had brought with her and the other, ripped one that she had just been wearing. If she simply cut the skirts off, she could make the upper halves into shirts with little adjustment. But if she was going to spend her days running around the island and sleeping in the dirt, even that would not be practical enough. Dresses of the sort she was used to wearing were too tight around the elbows, wrists and shoulders.

"What else is there to do on this island?" Ydana asked.

"We could go swimming."

The rest of the morning was spent flying to the lake and swimming, mostly in manticore form. Ydana was particularly amazed at Tara's ability to dive down and catch a fish, waving the silvery prey in her jaws. She tried to copy her friend and catch her own fish, but came up empty. But Tara was nice enough to share her kill.

The two ate together on a nearby rock. Though very few of the other manticores at the lake were in human form, Ydana took her human form anyway, to pick the bones out of the rest of the fish meat. Though she had eaten her prey bones and all before, she was not about to do the same with small, prickly fish bones.

Lying on the rock to dry off, she now saw the use of wearing such a small shirt, because it was drying off much more quickly than one of her dresses would have. Unbraiding her hair, she fanned her dark curls out on the rock to help them dry.

"How did you learn to fish like that?" she felt foolish asking such a question of someone in manticore form who couldn't answer.

"A lot of practice," Tara took her half human form to answer. Her hair was also wet, a few strands plastered to her face. "The only other prey we get on the island are rabbits, mice and other rodents. You can catch birds as well, though one usually needs to fly a bit of a distance from the island to catch any. And we can't hunt too much on the island, or else there will be too little prey left. So rather than flying down to the human world, some of us prefer to catch fish. There's still a limit on how much of that we can realistically do and still ensure that there are enough of them left, however. But every day, at least a few manticores will fly down below to catch larger prey."

"There's quite a bit that we have to bother the humans for, isn't there?" Ydana closed her eyes against the sunlight.

"I'm afraid so. We may be safe here, away from the humans, but we can't survive without venturing down to the human world sometimes."

Growing tired from so much sunlight and from having been awake all night, Ydana and Tara flew back to Tara's campsite and took a nap, their manticore forms taking up most of Tara's campsite area. Ydana did not know how long she slept, but when she awoke, she heard voices.

"I wouldn't wake her yet if I were you," Tara was saying. "She was pretty angry with you for not telling her, and I don't know if she still is."

"I hadn't exactly intended for her to find out that way, either," a familiar voice answered. Val.

Ydana kept her eyes closed, pretending to still be asleep.

"Honestly, Val, what did you think would happen?" Tara said. "Now she's convinced that you can't possibly like her. But I know you do, so why did you have to mess up so badly?"

"Tara, I think you're mistaken about who likes who here, because it's Ydana who is not interested in me. And while I am worried what mother will think of my turning so many sweet innocent humans into manticores when the first one should have worked out, I'm more concerned about the girl who has already faced so much danger and had her whole life uprooted because of me."

Tempted to open her eyes, Ydana couldn't help but wonder what Val meant by having turned 'so many' humans into manticores. Were there others besides Tara and herself?

But something else Val had just said was nagging at her even more. By saying 'it's Ydana who is not interested,' Val had implied that she was, in fact, interested in her. But that could hardly be true, and Ydana was tempted to dismiss it as her wanting Tara to think she cared more for Ydana than she truly did.

"I think you're still blaming yourself for what happened to Mitra," Tara said after a pause.

"You never even met Mitra, so you can hardly say that."

"And you're comparing Ydana to her," Tara was undeterred by Val interrupting her. "From what you've told me, Mitra was more the type to make her feelings perfectly clear. Ydana has probably never done such a thing in her life. Now I'm going hunting, and you can either talk to her, or just watch her until I get back."

When Ydana felt the breeze from wings flapping, she knew that Tara had taken off. Hearing only complete silence, she wondered if Val had flown after her, but kept her eyes shut in case she was still close by.

The crunch of leaves confirmed that she was still at the campsite, and it sounded like she was taking a step towards Ydana's pile of belongings. Closing her eyes more tightly, she heard Val pick up a book and begin turning pages.

"How much longer are you going to pretend to be sleeping?"

Her voice broke the silence, and Ydana breathed in sharply.

"Even if I had still thought you were asleep, that gave you away," Val said. "If you're still angry with me, I should tell you how sorry I am. I didn't think for a moment that you would be, and...I suppose I should have thought of that. You don't have to say anything if you don't want to, and you don't even have to forgive me. But..."

Ydana heard her placing the book back on top of the others.

"This one-sided conversation is getting awfully boring," she said. "I would really appreciate some input from you."

Taking her human form, Ydana sat up. Val was sitting, fully human and wearing only a shirt, trousers and boots, on a log next to Ydana's books. If she was surprised to find Ydana dressed like Tara with her hair loose from its usual braids, she didn't show it.

"I'm not angry," Ydana said quickly. "Not at all. Your highness. Or whatever they call you here."

"You don't need to address me as any title," Val's lips turned upwards into a smile.

"What do they call your parents? The Podishah and Malake? Or do they call them The King and Queen like in Grusrecia?"

Val simply laughed to himself before answering.

"To you, they are Soheila and Vash, and they are actually also simply a princess and her consort. My grandmother is the Ruling Lady, as we call her."

"What's your grandfather, then? The Ruling Lord?"

"The Advisor," Val answered. "We only have one Ruler at a time. Their partner, if they have one, is second to them in decision making."

Ydana scratched her head. She had not expected the ruling system of the manticores to be so different from the way it worked in Hashem.

"All of the manticores who were not human at one point, such as myself, are all related, as I have mentioned," Val continued to explain. "So, we are the equivalent of the nobility, you might say, though we probably make up nearly a third of the manticore population. So not every manticore who was originally a manticore has an equal place in the government. Only those most closely related to the Ruling Lady are princes and princesses. As a direct descendent of the Ruling Lady, I am also in line to be the Ruling Lady, after my mother."

Still trying to wrap her brain around the manticores' complex political system, Ydana could think of nothing to say as she sat up further.

"Anyway, I'm...glad you're not angry," Val was struggling to fill the silence. "And that you are getting along with Tara. She's my best friend, and usually I'm the only one she gets along with."

"You should, if you're the one who stung her," Ydana looked straight into her eyes as she hesitated to ask the question she most wanted to. "How many people have you stung before?"

"Three, counting you."

So, this Mitra person he and Tara had been talking about must have been another manticore like she had surmised.

"Are you still friends with the third one?"

Val shook her head. "I'm afraid not. I don't know how much of my conversation with Tara you heard, but her name was Mitra. She...let's just hope you never meet her."

She was still alive? Though Ydana was curious about this other manticore that had been a supposed romantic partner of Val's, she did not want to ask her anything else about her. Especially if she still lived. If Val was withholding information, it was most likely because she didn't want to talk about whatever happened.

"As I said before, you're my favorite of everyone I've stung," Val smiled again. "And I really do hope you're the last, whether you ever decide that I'm worthy of you that way or not."

"I..." Ydana felt a blush creep to her cheeks, and hoped that Val didn't notice. "It's not that I don't...I mean, I'll think about it."

"Don't think about it, Ydana," Val got to her feet and closed the distance between them. To Ydana's surprise, she offered her a hand and pulled her to her feet. "If you're interested in me that way, you know."

"It's not that I'm...not. But there was someone, before."

"There was?" Val tucked a strand of Ydana's hair behind her ear. "I had no idea."

Ydana could only nod.

"Here I've been so worried about myself, when you've been heartbroken all this time."

"It's not that I was heartbroken, exactly," Ydana shook her head. Her last encounter with Sasha already felt like months ago, and it felt strange to think about him again, but she did feel as if there were questions left unanswered where he was concerned. "We weren't in love, but he did seem to care about me, despite my being a manticore, and yet he was awfully quick to give up on me once his parents changed their minds and forbid him to marry me like he had planned."

"I'm so sorry," Val embraced her. "He's an idiot, and he will probably end up with some boring person his parents decide on."

Behind Val, Tara landed onto the ground, a rabbit in her jaws. To Ydana's surprise, Val did not take Tara's arrival as her cue to release Ydana from her embrace.

"I see you two have gotten somewhere," Tara wasted no time teasing them once she took her half-human form.

"And we're about to go somewhere else," Val turned to face her friend, a half-smile dancing across her face, before turning back to Ydana. "That is, if you're coming with me. You're more than welcome to stay here and bother Tara, but I imagine I would miss you too much."

Ydana simply nodded, embarrassed at her inability to wipe the smile from her face.

"Would you like some help packing?" Val turned away from her and turned to her pile of books.

"I can manage," she nervously shoved the books and clothing into her pillowcase, getting some leaves into it by mistake. It crossed her mind to leave them all there, but Tara's remark about them being valuable made her hesitate. It was probably best to take enough with her that she would be able to trade one if needed. "Tara, do you want some books? You helped me, after all."

"Leave me whichever one you think I'd enjoy the most," Tara said. "Especially if it was published in the last 50 years."

Ydana left half of her pile of books next to Tara's belongings, leaving only the classics in her sack. "You can borrow all of these. And then keep whichever ones are your favorites."

"And in return, you can keep that outfit," Tara smirked. "You look great."

Before Ydana could reply, Val took the sack of Ydana's meager belongings from her and hoisted it over her shoulder.

"We'll see you later, Tara," Val took her half-manticore form, spread her batlike wings, and took off into the air.

In her manticore form, Ydana launched herself into the air after her. Though she had seen much of the island, she had a feeling that very little of it would prepare her for where she and Val were going next.

## CHAPTER ELEVEN

As they flew, Val pointed out different landmarks. Ydana thought it would be frustrating to fly alongside someone who was able to take a half human form and, thusly, talk while she couldn't, but she was happy just to find out more about the island. Around them flew other manticores, both in fully manticore forms, and others halfway between the two.

Soon, Ydana spotted Val's dwelling in the distance, remembering it from when it had been pointed out to her that morning. As they flew closer, she saw that it had a flat roof, complete with what looked like a window that led down inside.

"What happened, Val? Did you make a friend down there in the human world again?" a manticore waiting on Val's rooftop said in a teasing voice. Her messy curls were longer than Tara's and more tangled, but she wore a blue headband to keep her tresses away from her young face. Ydana noticed that this manticore had bat wings like Val's, marking her as one who had been born a manticore.

"Vaja, I said you could have *some* of the venison, not half!" Val laughed as she landed. Though she was scolding her friend, her tone had a lightheartedness to it, as if she were amused by what Vaja had done. "I went down below to hunt that just for Ydana!"

Ydana noticed that between them was a deer, with several bites taken out of it.

"Oh, and is this *Ydana* worth hunting a deer for? Third time's the charm, right?"

The way Vaja put an extra emphasis on Ydana's name made Ydana feel slightly nervous about having a Grusrecian name on an island where most manticores were fully Hashemi.

"There's no need to be mean, Vaja," a male manticore dropped to the ground next to her, folding his bat wings behind him. He looked to be about the same age as Val and Vaja, but one could never tell with manticores, it would seem. "It's not Val's problem if she can't find the right human."

"Ydana, these are my cousins Dara and Vaja," Val acted as if they had said nothing. "They're not likely to go anywhere until this deer is gone, so you had better start eating."

Feeling awkward about taking the first bite, Ydana waited until the three of them had transformed to full manticores and were all bent over the deer. By the time she had eaten her fill, Val and her cousins were done eating and had already gotten back to talking.

"Grandmother still doesn't know about her, does she?" Dara tilted his head in Ydana's direction. Though in his human form, he sat on the edge of the flat rooftop, as if he had no fear of falling over the edge. Ydana guessed that most manticores didn't.

"The only one Ydana has met so far is Tara," Val said.

"Oh no, the new girl meets the last one you chose!" Vaja laughed. "How did that go?"

"They're best friends now," Val seemed to be wishing her cousins would hurry and leave. "Nothing to worry about."

"Oh, thank goodness! I would have hated to miss that meeting if some kind of fight had taken place. It's almost sad how little of that we get around here."

"I'm glad we have less drama than the humans do," Dara said. "It's nice to be able to find someone and know they're the one you're supposed to end up with. Well, in most cases, I guess. What I mean is that I'm glad to know that Misha and I will always have each other, and that she's so unlikely to leave and find someone else."

Finishing off her last bite, Ydana finally took her human form.

"I'm sorry I didn't say hello earlier," she eyed the pair of them. "I haven't figured out how to talk and fly. You know how it is."

"We certainly do," Dara seemed surprised at Ydana's human form, perhaps because she was already wearing clothing more typical of a manticore. "It takes us several years as cubs before we are able to take that form. Human form is a bit easier, but even that takes a lot of concentration at first."

Ydana had never considered the possibility that the manticores who were born as such had to learn to shift to their human forms.

While she was still deep in thought about how different a manticore who had been born as such was from one who had been human, Vaja and Dara bid their farewells and flew away, leaving Ydana and Val alone.

"What's wrong?" Val came to stand beside her.

"Nothing," Ydana shook her head. "I was only thinking about how different I am from the rest of you."

"That's to be expected, seeing as you are new to being a manticore."

"But which one am I really? Am I this form, or my manticore form?"

"Both, of course," Val said. "I consider my manticore form my true form, and when I look at you, I also think of that as your true form as well. But you were born human, and were raised by humans, and you have every right to consider your human form the true one. But of course, we are both. If part of us weren't also human, we would have no need of a human form at all."

Picking Ydana's sack of books up, Val led her towards the opening in the floor of the rooftop. Ydana took comfort in the fact that it was only small enough for a human, so she was not expecting a sudden drop down. Yet once she entered, she was surprised to find that there was a spiral staircase leading through the second story of the dwelling, presumably to the one below, though Ydana could see very little of the ground floor through the hole in the ground that the staircase went through.

"We're home," Val jumped over the railing to land on her feet on the ground below. "What do you think?"

Large windows (without any glass, as the manticores no doubt lacked a way to make glass on their island) allowed plenty of light in, to illuminate the paintings on the walls and the books on the room's lone bookshelf. The tomes gracing the shelves looked much older than the books that Ydana had brought with her from home. On one of the shelves lay a few knives and daggers, and a quiver of arrows. A bow and a spear leaned against the bookshelf.

The stone floor was covered in dust, but the room was otherwise devoid of any debris or clutter, and the only piece of furniture was a bed in one corner that looked like a shapeless pile of straw wrapped in animal skins. Covering it was a blanket of furs.

The room's only other adornment was a series of perfectly rectangular holes carved into the stone wall near the bed, some of which held folded clothing. One of them held several water skins and gourds. With only one lake on the island, Ydana could see the need for storing water containers nearby.

"It's…"

"I know it's hardly as immaculate as you're used to down among the humans, but we have limited resources on our small island," Val extended a hand to her and led her down the last few stairs.

"No, it's beautiful," Ydana looked around the room at everything but Val. "I was only thinking that you don't own very much."

"We don't need very much around here," she went to one of the rectangular holes in the wall, which Ydana noticed was empty, and placed the sack of Ydana's belongings inside. "This one's for you."

"Thank you," Ydana smiled nervously. "And I'm sorry to be such a bother."

"You're hardly that," Val crossed the room to stand with her. "I'm glad you're here. Why would you think your presence would bother me?"

"It seemed as if your cousins were making fun of you for having stung yet another person. I hate to be the source of that."

"You aren't," she put a hand to her face and stroked her cheek. "They would be saying that whether you were here or not. And you mean so much more to me than what other people think. Besides, I'm actually glad that the first human I stung didn't work out. It's much more fun this way, and I've never seen that as a bad thing."

Whether or not Val truly had feelings for her, which Ydana still thought too good to be true, she seemed to care more about her than anyone else. Looking into her eyes, Ydana found so much adoration for her, but she was still too afraid to simply assume that her friend felt something.

## CHAPTER TWELVE

The view from the boulder was just as spectacular as the sun set. Because they were looking in the opposite direction, Val and Tara pointed out different landmarks than they had that morning. She learned where the library was, as well as the largest clearing.

"And that's the house that my mother and father live in," Val pointed to another stone dwelling that looked similar to her own.

"Where does your grandmother live?" Ydana asked. "The Ruling Lady's house must be spectacular."

"It can't be seen from here," Val said. "It's deep in the woods, and not as tall. You will likely be seeing it soon. I'm sure our arrival will reach my grandmother's ears very soon, if she hasn't heard about you already."

"When are you taking Ydana to meet your parents?" Tara asked. "It's only a matter of time before they'll summon you and demand to know why you waited so long to see them."

"After this," Val said.

Ydana nearly jumped at her words, and turned to face her, eyes wide.

"So soon? Should I change into something nicer? I hardly want to offend them by showing up like this," she pointed to her bare stomach.

"You look great," Val moved closer to her so that their arms were touching, making Ydana's stomach flip over. "We have no dress code here like the humans do."

"Then why did you feel the need to put on a proper shirt?" Ydana teased her. The white shirt she had put on covered more than Ydana's or Tara's.

"Because I expect that we will be speaking with them in human form. If we were meeting with them in our in-between forms, I would still not have donned a nice shirt."

"Don't worry, Ydana, they're very nice," Tara spoke up, having seemingly sensed Ydana's anxiety at meeting Val's parents.

It wasn't that Ydana was afraid they would not like her. If Val's parents were anything like their daughter, she had suspected they would be perfectly nice people. But if the welcome from Val's cousins was anything to go by, Ydana was sure there would be others who would expect her and Val to be a couple. But that was hardly something she could control if she was not sure how Val felt.

As soon as the sun had set, Ydana and Val bid farewell to Tara and flew straight towards the stone rooftop that they had seen from the boulder. More manticores were flying through the sky than there had been during the day, and Ydana tried to distract herself from the task ahead of her by counting how many of the other manticores had the batlike wings of those who were born manticores, and how many had bird wings.

Instead of landing on the roof of Val's parents' house, they came to stand in front of what Ydana considered the front door, on ground level. She would have at least expected a front door to be the right size for a human, but instead, it appeared to be meant for manticores to enter through. Curtains were the only thing keeping the door closed, for there was no true door in the doorway. Through the curtains, she could see the light from a fire.

Val let out a roar, the meaning of which Ydana could not begin to determine. Another roar answered from inside, and Val seemed to take this as her cue to enter. Ydana tentatively followed her in through the curtained doorway.

A fire was burning in a fire pit in the center of the room, lighting up the dwelling. Ydana was surprised to see a fire indoors, but she supposed it made sense to do on a stone floor with nothing flammable in sight. The smoke simply floated out through a high window. In front of the fire sat two manticores, who turned to face them.

"Mother, father," Val shifted to her human form and bowed. "It's wonderful to see you both."

Ydana followed her lead and bowed as soon as she shifted to her human form.

Both of the manticores stood up from the fire and took their human forms as well, their eyes on Ydana. Val's mother was, surprisingly, dressed similarly to Ydana, which made Ydana far less nervous about wearing something she considered informal. Her long hair was held away from her face by a bandana, similar to what Val's cousin Vaja had been wearing. Val's father was dressed just as simply, in a shirt and trousers. They both looked no older than 30 in their human forms.

"It's good to see you, Valida," her mother came forward to embrace her daughter, before turning to Ydana.

"This is Ydana," Val embraced her father as well, who was also eying Ydana. Evidently, she didn't need to say anything more for them to know who Ydana was or why she was in their home.

"Come sit by the fire, both of you," Val's father beckoned them back to the fire. "I will get some tea started."

"Tea?" Ydana couldn't help but whisper. The very idea that something so normal for the humans in Hashem could exist among the manticores surprised her.

Val's father fetched a tea kettle from one corner of the room, poured water from a water skin into it, and set it on top of the fire, where it sat on two sticks, just above the flames.

"Welcome, Ydana," Val's mother embraced her and held her at arm's length as if Ydana were a relative she simply had not seen in a year. "Vash and I are so excited to meet you. What do you think of our island?"

"It's…nice," Ydana immediately cursed her inability to think of anything to say in social situations.

She took a seat by the fire, between Val and Soheila, while Vash brought four teacups out from a hole in the wall similar to the ones at Val's house, having filled each one with tea leaves.

"How is it possible that you have tea here?" Ydana asked.

"We grow the leaves, of course," Vash sat across from Ydana and Val, on the other side of Soheila. "A long time ago, someone must have decided that tea was too good not to have our own supply of."

"Has Valida explained the rules of hunting on the island?" Soheila asked, again using what was presumably Val's full name.

"Tara told me that we can only hunt some of the prey on the island to make sure there are enough animals left to sustain the population," Ydana hoped that was what Soheila was referring to.

"You've already met Tara?" Soheila looked surprised. "How long have you been here so far?"

"Only since sunrise."

Once the water in the tea kettle was deemed hot enough, the four of them sipped their tea while talking. At Soheila's request, Ydana recounted what she had done on the island so far, how she had met Val, and the events that followed. Ydana left out everything about Sasha, and only told bits and pieces of her time at the Meacham Academy. Val and her parents hardly needed to know how mean the other girls there had been and how terribly she had suffered through the manticore-specific lessons, but she made sure to mention what had happened to Misty.

"I wonder who stung her, and if they're still alive," Soheila wondered. "It's impossible for a manticore not to be able to find a person they stung, even if they go to live somewhere else."

"I'm curious about where she is now," Vash said. "I hope she got away alright, and that she finds her way here."

"Me too," Ydana looked down at her tea. She hoped that she would see Misty again, or at least find out where she was. "Do you know anything about the manticore hunters? Who are they? Where are they headquartered? Maybe we can stop them."

"Very little is known," Soheila began to explain. "We know that, though they can't very well kill us, they do something to their weapons to keep us from transforming. We don't, however, have any knowledge of what that may be. Anything else we have discovered before, such as where they are headquartered, changes all the time."

"There has to be a way, if you've discovered their headquarters before," Ydana contemplated. "With enough of us, we can stop them."

Beside her, Val stiffened.

"Don't think about that, Ydana," Soheila said more harshly than she had said anything before. "Stay safe on this island, or anywhere else, rather than go after the manticore hunters. You don't know how dangerous they are. If anything were to happen to you, we would all feel horrible, and it would destroy my daughter."

It took Ydana a moment to realize that by 'my daughter,' she meant Val. She could hardly correct Soheila and say that she didn't mean quite so much to Val as they thought, for fear of disappointing them.

"I'm afraid it's true," Val whispered in her ear, sending shivers down her spine. "I'd hate for anything to happen to you."

"I won't do anything rash," Ydana assured them.

Tea time continued on a lighter note after that. Val asked her parents to tell story after story for Ydana, and they asked her for news of the human world, and what had changed since they were last among the humans. It had been several decades since they had last set foot in Hashem, or any human country, and were surprised to hear that so many Grusrecians were living in Hashem and adopting aspects of Hashemi culture.

Ydana was fascinated by what Val's parents knew and didn't know about the current Hashemi culture because it had been so long since they had had any update. From the ongoing conversation, Ydana surmised that there had been manticore spies among the humans every once in awhile, but that the need for that had dwindled as the decades wore on, and the manticores felt more of a need to stay separate from the humans.

Though Ydana had been made to tell the story of how she and Val had met, Soheila and Vash never shared the story of how they met. Even when Val had asked them to tell Ydana stories about when Vash had first come to the island after he had turned, they pointedly left out anything having to do with the circumstances under which he had turned. Ydana guessed that it was too painful of a memory, if her own experience was anything to go by.

"It's about time my mother met Ydana, don't you think, Valida?" Soheila asked her daughter.

"Mother, I'm not sure if Ydana is ready for that," she stood up and followed her mother outside. "She has only been here for a day."

"You're going to meet her now, whether you're ready or not," Vash said to Ydana. "I can already tell who's winning that argument. But don't worry, the Ruling Lady is only slightly intimidating. The previous Ruling Lady absolutely hated me, but this one did not, surprisingly."

"Why 'surprisingly'?" Ydana asked.

"I caused a few bad things to happen back down in the human world. I'll explain later."

Once Val and Soheila returned, Val looked defeated as she sat back down by the fire. Soheila asked Ydana to come with her, and Ydana reluctantly followed her upstairs, to a bedroom floor that looked much like the one at Val's house, with a bed of straw and fur, and meager belongings adorning the walls and floor.

"Try this on," Soheila handed Ydana a shirt that was just as short as the one she had on, only it was blue, and made of silk, with sleeves that started part of the way down her arms, leaving her shoulders bare. Once Ydana put it on over her other shirt, she and Soheila went back downstairs where Vash and Val were putting the fire out.

"She's not that bad, I promise," Val whispered in her ear. "I'm sure she will find you as incredible as I do."

Ydana knew she was just trying to make her feel less nervous, and tried to smile encouragingly at her. Val gave her a worried look, which let her know that it did not have the desired effect.

Trying to think of anything but the meeting that was about to happen, Ydana once again busied herself with watching the other manticores in the sky as she flew. She hardly paid any attention to where it was, she was following Val and her parents, and was surprised when they began flying through the woods, moving slowly so as to dodge any trees in the way.

They landed at one end of the lake, far away from where she and Tara had swum. In front of them was a stone dwelling similar to the ones that Val and his parents lived in, only this one was carved into one side of a boulder. A curtain of vines covered the windows and doors, and two guards, both female and both with bat wings, in their in-between forms, stood on either side of the door with spears in their hands.

Val and her parents shifted to their in-between forms, and Ydana followed them to the doorway. She half expected the guards to wonder why she was still in manticore form, but they simply bowed upon recognizing Val and her parents.

Inside the stone fortress, torches lined the staircase that led up to the throne, illuminating it, and casting an eerie light onto the two guards who stood next to the throne, and the throne's occupant.

The Ruling Lady looked younger than middle age, with only a few wrinkles on her face, and hard eyes that had seen too much. Her dark hair bore not a streak of grey, and Ydana began wondering if manticores even began getting grey hairs no matter how old they were.

Despite sitting while the two guards next to her were standing, Val's grandmother looked larger than them. This was one of the few times Ydana had seen a female manticore next to a male, and the size difference was obvious. And yet she made herself look even larger with a throne that was several feet above where the guards stood.

Ydana would have been unnerved had the Ruling Lady's eyes been on her, but they were on another manticore, who stood before the throne and bowed, placing the dead deer she carried onto the floor.

"You're late." Her voice was iron.

"I apologize for my tardiness, your majesty," the manticore groveled. "It was only to bring you the largest prey…"

"Silence," she said simply, though it felt as if her voice echoed around the room.

The manticore stared up at her.

"Now get out," she said, before turning to her new visitors.

As soon as the hunter made his hasty exit and one of the guards made his way down the staircase to fetch the dead deer, Val's mother led the way to the throne, where she stood before the staircase.

"Your majesty," she bowed.

"Soheila," the Ruling Lady roared her daughter's name rather than said it, and Ydana was surprised that she understood it as a name. She waited for the Ruling Lady to say more. She did not.

"This is Ydana," Soheila did not need to point to her, seeing as the Ruling Lady could see who the newcomer in her midst was. "She is Valida's chosen."

The words made Ydana's fur stand up. Did Soheila really have to say she was Val's 'chosen' as if she were the only one?

"I see. Ydana," she was either addressing Ydana, or tasting the unusual name on her tongue. "That's an unusual name. Are you a Grusrecian?"

Ydana was not sure whether she was more surprised that the Ruling Lady was addressing her directly, or that she chose such a strange thing to be surprised about. Never before had her body been so unwilling to return to human form, but she did.

"I'm Hashemi, your majesty. My mother is Grusrecian."

"And do you believe that my granddaughter did the correct thing by choosing you?" the Ruling Lady's eyes bore into hers, and it took all of Ydana's willpower not to look away.

"Your Majesty, I..." Ydana had not been expecting that question. "I am glad that she chose me."

"Are you?" The Ruling Lady's face took on as confused of an expression as such a terrifying woman could.

"I suppose I...I sort of...hated her for it at first, because of the way I had constantly been treated as a manticore, but now that I am not among the humans any longer, things are different." Ydana immediately felt like a fool for giving such a long-winded answer. Surely the Ruling Lady wouldn't want her granddaughter to have chosen someone who prattles on and on about nothing.

"And Valida," the Ruling Lady addressed her granddaughter for the first time. "Will this be the last time you choose?"

"Of course," Val did not hesitate.

To Ydana's astonishment, the Ruling Lady smiled.

"Are you saying that because you are hoping not to sting any more humans, or because this girl is the one who will stay with you?"

"Grandmother, Ydana has only just arrived, and she hasn't..."

"Answer the question," her voice did not echo this time.

For a moment, no one said anything. Ydana did not need to look at Val to see the uncertainty radiating off of her. She knew that Val was avoiding looking at her, either.

"Yes," Ydana shocked herself by speaking up. "I am staying, and if Val...I mean Valida...will have me, then I am 'the one', as you say."

Immediately, her cheeks burned, and she took her manticore form too quickly, so that no one could read her face expressions. She had thought saying that she would stay if Val would have her was a safe answer, seeing as she was still unsure how Val felt and did not want to assume.

"Then I wish you the best. You may go."

The four of them exited the stone fortress, and the cool night air felt good blowing through Ydana's mane. She still felt mortified by most of what she had told the Ruling Lady. Val could hardly be interested in her now, no matter what she had said at Tara's campsite. She must have thought Ydana a blithering idiot for answering the question for her. Or worse, perhaps she thought her a little girl blindly in love with her. She shook her head, as if she could shake the thoughts out.

Once they had left that part of the forest and taken off into the air, Val's parents took their in-between forms and began talking. From the little that Ydana could hear from behind them with the wind whistling by, she guessed that they were discussing how that meeting had gone. She wished she could better hear what they were saying, but did not want to eavesdrop.

Still in manticore form, Val flew beside her. She could feel her eyes on her, but she kept her gaze straight ahead until they came to land on Val's parents' rooftop. Ydana stayed in manticore form as the others said their farewells. Taking her human form long enough to take off the shirt she had borrowed from Soheila and hand it back to her proved difficult, and she felt the physical effects of her embarrassment, such as blood rushing to her face, as soon as she did so. Embracing Vash and Soheila briefly, she went straight back to manticore form.

She was relieved to land on Val's rooftop afterwards, and yet it took all of Ydana's willpower to transform back into a human and follow Val through the door in the roof and down the stairs.

"Are you alright?" Val asked when she still had not spoken.

Ydana nodded.

"Did you mean what you said about your feelings?" Val reached the bottom step and extended a hand to help Ydana down the last few steps.

"I..." she took her hand. "I'm sorry, Val. You can ignore what I said if you want to. It doesn't matter to me."

"It matters to me," Val held her hand tightly in hers. "I have loved you since we first met at the party, and I have been hoping ever since then that you felt the same."

"But before I went to boarding school, you said that it wouldn't bother you in the least if I didn't feel the same. That's why I thought you weren't interested in me."

"Would I have followed you to the boarding school so quickly if I didn't care?" she smiled, making Ydana feel as if she would melt.

With a confidence she did not know she possessed, Ydana leaned forward and kissed her. For a moment, she was shocked at what she had done, and wondered if she should draw back, but Val eagerly kissed her back, embracing her.

It was nothing like the time Sasha had kissed her. This time, she could feel how much love Val felt for her, that she truly cared. She leaned into her embrace and wished that she would never let her go.

## CHAPTER THIRTEEN

      Lord Azra had hardly left his study in days. As soon as Lady Ylaine had told him of Ydana's escape from the Academy, he had gone home ahead of her and Victor, and resumed his search for the floating island that was home to the manticores.
      Every trip he had taken over the past twelve years, whether business related or simply a social call, was really a search for the island that was only rumored to exist. Even when Lady Ylaine insisted that Victor was old enough to accompany him, not knowing the true nature of his travels, Lord Azra only allowed him to come during the time of year when the weather would be too cloudy for the island to be seen. Once Victor was able to oversee their operations on his own, Lord Azra left him to do that while he himself resumed the search for the island, without his stepson's knowledge.

After leaving the Grusrecian border when Ylaine and Victor were still visiting with Lady Elvira, he searched again for the island. He had studied where it was rumored to have been seen over the past few centuries, visiting the areas around those same places repeatedly, but all he found were small floating islands, much too miniscule for even one manticore to live on, let alone most of their population.

There had been times when he wondered what the point was of finding the island, especially when his daughter had not yet turned, and he sometimes stopped looking for it altogether. After all, there had supposedly been manticore hunters looking for it for centuries. And he had no plan for when he did find it. But every time Ydana threw an uncharacteristic temper tantrum or chased a mouse or insect was a reminder to Lord Azra that he had to continue his search.

Ydana's leaving the Meacham Academy with manticore hunters on her tail made him the most desperate he had ever been to find the island. He had not even bothered to get a full night's sleep since. He took notes on every book he had on the subject of manticores, trying to find something, anything that would give him a clue he had not discovered previously. Behind some of the more typical books in his study lay an entire row of books about manticores, with illustrations on the covers of lions with human faces. Azra wondered, on occasion, if this was simply the best way to depict that manticores could appear human, or if they could, indeed, appear as a lion while only their faces remained human.

"Azra, honestly, you can't keep up like this," Ylaine made her way into the study without bothering to knock. "Ydana is gone, and she did not get captured by the manticore hunters, I'm quite sure."

"I have to know where she is," Azra flipped through the index of his most recently acquired book on manticores. He had only just had it delivered as soon as Ydana had turned. "I can't accept that I will never see my daughter again. It's important for me to know where she is."

"Will you please hurry and get dressed. If you're not at Lord Warrington's son's engagement party, people will start to talk. It is a cousin of yours he's marrying, after all."

"Then I will leave again, and they will know that I am away on business," Azra still did not look up from his book.

The Veshteh-Blanchard family had agreed to pretend that Ydana was still at the Meacham Academy and that nothing was amiss. They had agreed that this was best for Ydana's safety and their own. Azra did not know how the manticore hunters worked, and how many of them were after Ydana, but certainly she would be in more danger if she was known to have escaped the Meacham Academy.

"You have to come to the party, or else it would look poorly on Victor and Elvira," Ylaine's mention of Elvira reminded Azra that Victor's fiancée was indeed staying with them, because he had all but forgotten that she was there.

With a sigh, Azra nodded.

On their way to the party, all Azra could think about was Ydana. If he was stepping away from his desk for the evening, he had to at least keep his ears open for anything concerning manticores.

"What a quaint little window display," Elvira looked out the window of the carriage as they passed someone's house. "We should set up something like that when we get our own house. No one in Grusrecia does that, so we will be setting a trend."

"Yes, everyone has those here," Victor explained.

Azra had to stop himself from rolling his eyes. Why didn't Victor explain that the window display is for devotees of Mahsa, the goddess that most Hashemi prayed to? Though Azra no longer practiced any sort of religion, his family had mostly been devotees of Mahsa, and to hear his future daughter in law refer to a statuette of her as simply a quaint window display, and his stepson not correct her, was enough to make him want to jump out of the carriage and go home.

Elvira was still chattering endlessly and displaying her ignorance of Hashemi culture when they arrived at the ball. Stepping out of the carriage first, Azra offered his arm to Ylaine, who accompanied him to the door, and handed their invitations to the doorman. Immediately, Ylaine was seized by two ladies, one Hashemi and one Grusrecian, who she began chatting with, leaving Azra to his own devices.

It had been quite some time since Azra had bothered to attend a gathering of any kind hosted by any of the Grusrecian nobles. There was still plenty of Hashemi food and decorations, and plenty of Hashemi guests, yet Azra experienced culture shock every time.

For every woman wearing a normal Hashemi dress, there was someone else whose petticoats were so large that anyone talking to them had to stand a good distance away. For every piece of bread on the table of appetizers that had khoreshte bademjoon spread on it, there was another with a garish pile of sauce and what looked like very crusty bright red beans.

"Lord Azra, how nice to see you."

Azra turned to find Lord Warrington's son, Sasha. It was then that he recalled that this had been the boy who had wanted to marry Ydana.

"Sasha, congratulations on your engagement," he clapped the boy's hand in both of his own before letting go. "And your soon-to-be royal status."

"Well, I don't know about that."

"Within a year, they're bound to officially make you a prince, Grusrecian or not."

Anyone marrying into the Hashemi royal family was not automatically coronated. Instead, they had to demonstrate a certain capability before they were selected to become a prince or princess.

"Perhaps, but...how is Ydana?" Sasha lowered his voice.

The question surprised Azra, and for a moment, he struggled with what to tell the boy. Part of him wanted to let him know what happened, seeing as Ydana may want him to know. But at the same time, he had given Ylaine his word that he would stick to their story.

"She is attending school at the Meacham Academy for Young Women."

"Oh, I see," Sahsa's face expression was a mixture of relief and disappointment, and Azra could not tell which it was. "I hope she is at least having a nice time there."

"She is learning a lot," Azra nodded. Lying had never come easily to him, but it was even more difficult with someone who knew Ydana well enough to potentially smell a lie.

"I imagine she's safest there," Sasha continued. "I hear that there are manticore hunters about, and…let's just say that ever since Ydana turned, I have been hoping for cloudy weather to impede their search for the mantiores' island."

"Me too," Azra said, too quickly.

A normal person would have inquired further about manticore hunters or otherwise treated them as something strange. Saying 'me too' as if their existence was common knowledge would stand out as strange behavior indeed. Azra kept his face expression as neutral as possible, in the hopes that Sasha would not think anything of his casual reaction to the term 'manticore hunters'.

If he thought it was strange that Azra knew of them, Azra thought it all the more unusual that Sasha would know of such a thing. Surely the family that Sasha was marrying into hadn't been so quick to let him in on their secrets when it came to hunting manticores. But if they had not, why else would Sasha so easily mention the subject to Azra, who had once been part of that family.

"It was nice to see you, Sasha," Azra clapped him on the shoulder and wandered into the crowd, hoping to avoid being followed.

Though it was somewhat chilly, he felt stifled. All sorts of questions ran through his mind about where the island was and how he could lead the manticore hunters away from it once he found out. His first step should be to talk to Sasha again once he was calm, but first, he wanted to get some fresh air.

Once he reached the back door, he pushed it open, perhaps too hastily. A few people standing outside in the garden greeted him, and he managed a brief hello before wandering to a more secluded section of the garden.

No sooner had he taken a deep breath, than he felt something hit him on the back of the head, and everything went black.

## CHAPTER FOURTEEN

Sasha hastily donned his mask as his father woke Lord Azra with smelling salts. The mask covered his entire head, leaving holes for his eyes just big enough for him to see through, and his disguise was completed by a black, unrecognizable cloak that hid his clothing from view. He hardly saw the point of wearing a disguise, for Lord Azra would surely recognize both his and his father's voices.

He had also wondered why they couldn't simply have someone else interrogate Lord Azra. His father's argument had been that if Lord Azra recognized them, he would be unable to prove it, seeing as no sensible person would be gone from his own party. They had two other interrogators standing by in case this took longer than Sasha and Lord Warrington could afford to be absent from the party.

"Where are the manticores?" Lord Warrington barked. "Where is their island?"

"I don't know," Lord Azra looked weary.

"What has your research shown you? The sooner you answer, the sooner we can let you go back to the party."

"The party?" Lord Azra sat up, suddenly. "Where is my wife? Is she alright?"

"Answer the question!"

"Not until I know she's alright! And my son as well!"

"They're fine," Sasha spoke up, lowering his voice so as to disguise it. His father looked back at him, and Sasha was sure he was glaring daggers at him through the mask.

"Now answer the question!" Lord Warrington turned back towards Lord Azra. "Where is the island?"

"I honestly don't know," Lord Azra said with a sigh. "It makes no difference how long you keep me here. I have no information about where it could be."

Lord Warrington signaled for one of the other two interrogators present, one of the Podishah's manticore hunter lackeys, to step forward, while he himself pulled Sasha away.

"You are clearly not ready for such things, boy," Lord Warrington whispered in Sasha's ear. "You must shape up if you are to be a manticore hunter!"

"What has your research shown you?" the interrogator's voice sounded far away as Sasha and his father left the room. Lord Azra's response was too muffled for him to hear.

"What if I don't want to be a manticore hunter?" Sasha faced his father. "Did you ever think of that?"

"What you want doesn't matter!" his father whispered. "It's about keeping the innocent children of this kingdom from turning into monsters!"

"Ydana was no monster!"

"*Was* no monster," his father put the emphasis on 'was'. "Who knows what she is now. If we had been able to bring her to our side before she turned, then perhaps we could have tamed her. She could have helped us, and led us to the manticores. But when she turned sooner than we had expected, she ruined our plans."

"So *that's* why you wanted me to marry Ydana, and suddenly…didn't anymore?" Sasha was surprised. Though he had wondered why his parents had suddenly been unwilling to allow him to marry Ydana despite having always known she was a manticore, he had never expected them to have a plan for her.

"You need to forget about Ydana! She is one of them now!"

Sasha wanted to protest, to let his father know that Ydana was still his friend, that he would help her if she returned, but it was useless to argue. Ydana was long gone, and Sasha could never come back from knowing he was part of a family of manticore hunters. He was about to marry a manticore hunter, no less.

"I forgot about Ydana a long time ago. But I will never forget the way you made me betray her," Sasha turned away and went back to the ballroom.

After another half hour of socializing at the party, his thoughts still on Lord Azra being interrogated, Sasha was approached by Lady Ylaine.

"Sasha, how wonderful to see you! Have you seen my husband?"

"I saw him in the men's room not long ago," Sasha lied. "How is Ydana?"

"She's doing wonderfully at boarding school," Ylaine plastered her fake smile onto her face. "She has made several new friends, all wonderful young ladies, and she has even met a fellow."

"Has she?" Sasha knew she was lying, but he could hardly blame Lady Ylaine for trying to put forth what was, in her mind, the best image of her daughter. "That's great to hear. What is her favorite area of study?"

Feeling terrible, Sasha knew the best thing to do was to keep Lady Ylaine talking. The more questions he asked her, the less she would wonder where her husband had wandered off to, buying his interrogators time to find out what they could before sending him back to the party.

But that was not the only reason he had for asking more questions. He wanted to find out what the story really was with Ydana. If she truly had made friends, and especially a man she was interested in, Lord Azra would have mentioned that earlier.

Besides, Sasha knew Ydana well enough to know that she was far from a social butterfly. The odds of her having met a man and even made friends only a month into her time at boarding school were slim to none. And Sasha knew how manticores were treated.

"She's learning how to play the harp," Lady Ylaine answered. "I'm so proud of her."

"Has she made any plans to come home to visit?"

"She's having such a wonderful time there, that she is not thinking of visiting any time soon. But I'm sure she will decide to in the next few months."

"Well, that's nice to hear," Sasha could not listen to any more of her lies. "Send my regards to her in your next letter, would you?"

"Of course!" Lady Ylaine said with too wide of a smile.

"It was nice to see you."

He wandered only a little way before being stopped by guest after guest wanting to congratulate him. More people had wanted to speak to him while he was standing with his fiancée, Princess Sahar, because they wanted to be introduced to a princess, but a few people did still seek him out when he was by himself, giving him hardly a moment to breathe during the party.

Once the first few people he spoke to said their farewells, he came across someone who was not a guest, but Princess Sahar's cousin, Ashar. He was a cousin so many times removed that he did not even have the title of Prince.

"Sasha, quickly, come with me," he practically grasped Sasha by the sleeve and hauled him outside.

"What is it?"

"He told us where it isn't."

Sasha did not need to ask who 'he' or 'it' was.

"And?"

"I think we can assume where it *is*," Ashar lowered his voice to a whisper. "And I'm fairly certain our guest realized the same thing, though he didn't say."

"Where?" Sasha wished that Ashar would get to the point.

"Above Mount Sardar," Ashar said excitedly.

Sasha's eyes widened. It made perfect sense, for Mount Sardar was the tallest mountain in all of Hashem. It was so tall that only three people were known to have scaled it all the way to the top. And the sky above it was always so cloudy, that any island floating above it would not be seen.

"Perfect. My associates will confirm its location," said a new voice from behind Sasha.

He spun around to find Princess Sahar standing behind him. Her eyes were, as always, obscured by a veil that came down from her hairclip. Only now, the veil was blue, to match the dress she wore. By now, Sasha had seen her wear the same hairclip with a veil in several different colors, and she never went without it.

"Your highness, I hadn't realized you were there," Sasha put an arm around her as she stepped up to stand next to him. Though he felt awkward calling his fiancée by her title, he knew how much worse it would feel not to. He doubted that he would call her anything else, even after they were married.

"Anyway, we have let our guest go back to the party," Ashar said. "I highly doubt he will say anything. And even if he does, nobody will believe him."

"How are you going to confirm the island's location?" he asked Princess Sahar once Ashar had left them. "Furthermore, how can we even get there? We can't fly."

Princess Sahar did not say anything for a moment, and Sasha began wondering if she even knew how they would get to the island.

"We manticore hunters have our means," she finally said. "After all, we have spent centuries attempting to keep up with a creature that can fly. You have not seen our flying machines yet, have you?"

"Flying machines?" Sasha had never seen anything of the sort at his own house. "You mean…we *can* fly?"

"Most of the flying machines are small, and can seat one or two people, but there has been a large one in development for some time, and it was finally completed last year. But naturally, we have kept it a complete secret, as we can hardly allow the manticores to find out that we have it."

Every time Princess Sahar mentioned the manticores, her voice was filled with such hate. Sasha had guessed, for some time, that she had a real reason for wanting to hunt the manticores, more than his parents did.

"What did the manticores do to make you hate them so much?" Sasha asked.

"Why should they have done something to me specifically? They're unnatural creatures."

"My own brother was turned into a manticore and eventually taken away, and I don't hate them. I even had a friend who was a manticore, who I was planning to marry, knowing that she was a manticore," Sasha pointed out. "Clearly they must have done something worse to you than taking a family member. In fact, I find it odd that you hate them, yet you were happy to know that I had stood up for one."

Facing him, Princess Sahar lifted the veil from her eyes.

## CHAPTER FIFTEEN

With a yawn, Ydana awoke from her slumber. It was only when she stretched her paws in front of her that she realized she had changed into her manticore form in her sleep.

She had gone to sleep as a human every night since she had arrived on the island two weeks before, but woke up as a manticore most of the time. Val had told her that it was a sign of her being happier and more free than she had been in the human realm.

Reverting to her more familiar human form, she sank back against Val's fur.

"Hey," Val took her human form and put an arm around her. "How would you feel if I used you as a pillow?"

"I'd hardly care," Ydana laughed. "Your fur is so tangled and messy anyway. It isn't even soft."

"The only reason yours isn't like that is because you haven't spent as much time here as a manticore. Look how much more tangled your human hair is than mine." She tried to run her fingers through a strand of Ydana's hair, but found it too tangled.

Ydana couldn't help but laugh to herself. She had already cut her hair to just past shoulder length to keep it from becoming too tangled, yet that had appeared to only somewhat help. Meanwhile, Val's long hair remained as straight and as soft as ever.

"I have never felt this unattractive in my life," she rolled her eyes. "I'm not sure why you even…"

"Don't even say that," Val propped herself onto one arm and looked her in the eyes. "How can you even think such a thing?"

She gave her such a worried look, that Ydana almost felt terrible. It was as if Ydana had insulted Val, instead of herself.

"I…" she wasn't sure what to say. She couldn't very well apologize to her for a remark that wasn't directed at her.

"I can't believe you still think such things about yourself, Ydana. I have loved you ever since we officially met."

"But that's only because I'm the one you stung," Ydana said. "You didn't have any control over how you felt about me."

"And yet Tara and I are just friends," Val pointed out.

"A rare exception," Ydana shrugged. "What about the first one, Mitra? Weren't you in love with her?"

She felt almost relieved when Val didn't answer right away. Ever since she had first found out about Mitra, and that she was still alive somewhere, she had wondered why this Mitra woman had left, and if Val would have chosen to stay with her. But she had never been able to bring herself to ask either Val or Tara about her.

"It didn't work out with her," Val finally said. "It was doomed from the start."

"But weren't you…happy with her for at least a while?" Ydana was hesitant to ask, especially since she had never brought up Mitra in conversation before.

"I stung her by accident. She was a manticore hunter, and I had meant to kill her. When she turned instead, I tried to help her, and that's when…when we…"

Ydana wanted to finish her sentence for her, but she was unwilling to simply say anything about Val being in love with someone else. She didn't want her to say it either.

"And yet she left?"

"It didn't last long. At all. I know we don't keep track of time the same way humans do, but it may not have even been a year. She had been a manticore hunter, and she was doomed to hate us."

"Why hate you? Or rather…us," Ydana corrected herself.

"I wondered the same thing for a long time, but I have since stopped asking myself that. It shouldn't matter why a particular manticore hunter has such an issue with our kind, only that she does."

Before Ydana could decide what to say, a manticore flew in through the window, landing gracefully on the floor.

"Hello, you two," the manticore transformed into Tara's human form. "Sorry to interrupt, but I've been waiting way too long for you to show up."

Embarrassed, Ydana practically sprang from the bed.

"Tara, did you really have to surprise us like that?" Val was much calmer than Ydana.

"We were supposed to go below for hunting a while ago!" Tara scolded. "If the Ruling Lady doesn't get her food by the time the sun goes down, it's not me who will get the blame. If she even remembers that I exist."

From what she new of Val's grandmother, Ydana suspected that the Ruling Lady was too busy to pay attention to any manticores that used to be human.

Ydana had been down below to hunt larger game during her time on the island, but she was by herself with either Val or Tara, and only for fun or to bring something extra back for Val's parents. This would be her first time venturing below for prey specifically to feed the Ruling Lady, who never hunted her own game.

Soon, the three of them were racing through the clouds in manticore form, gliding down from the island towards the snowy mountain below. In front of her, she could see flakes of snow landing on Tara's and Val's fur.

What surprised Ydana was that they did not stop at the mountain. Instead, they continued down to the ground where the air was less cold. The farther away from the mountain they flew, the greener and less snowy the ground became. When Val and Tara separated, Ydana took that as her cue to separate from them as well.

Diving into a forest below, she dropped through the trees to crouch in the shadows. A few squirrels ran away from her, but she had not come here for the same sized prey she could easily find on the island.

Before long, a doe approached, and Ydana ignored her salivating long enough for the deer to come closer. While she did not want her prey to get close enough to catch her scent, she also didn't want to bungle the whole thing by pouncing too soon. She may have been fast, but a deer was certainly faster when surrounded by trees.

## Fire Consumes Us

When the deer was close enough, Ydana leapt from her hiding place. Startled, the deer bolted. But Ydana was prepared. Pouncing onto the deer, she sank her claws into its hind leg before tearing its throat out with her teeth. With the deer's blood spilling onto her, she began eating her fill as soon as the light left its eyes.

Though she hardly needed to eat the whole deer, she wanted to make the most of it before returning to the island where such a meal could not be found. So she ate until she couldn't anymore, before finding a new hiding place, away from the deer carcass.

She did not know how long it had been by the time she caught a second deer, this time to take back to the island with her, but the sky was growing dark. Flying up, her jaws around the dead deer's neck, she tore through the sky towards the mountains.

She spotted a glint of light in the dark sky ahead of her. With no time to wonder what it could be, she dove back down, flying lower to the ground as she came closer to it. If it was one of the flying machines that the manticore hunters had chased her with at the Meacham Academy, she could fight them. But part of her was too scared to try.

The deer carcass was heavy, and Ydana wondered how she would be able to keep from dropping it, without Val to help her, yet she flew on. She saw no sign of Val or Tara, yet she was sure that at least Val would have waited for her or come to find her, even if Tara had already taken her kill back to the island.

Diving back into the woods, Ydana found a hiding place for the dead deer before flying back up again, unburdened by her kill. As she came closer to the flying machine, she saw that it was not the small two-seater that she had seen the manticore hunters use before. This one was flying much more slowly, with wings that beat more steadily, more to guide the machine than to keep it up in the air. From as far away as she was, she could not tell what was powering it, but the largest part of it was a balloon of air, with the actual body of the machine taking up less space, underneath the balloon.

Staying far enough away from the flying machine that she could barely see its lights, she followed it. Just when she decided that it was unlikely to be manticore hunters after all, she realized that it was headed for the mountain range, where it was sure to get close to the island.

## CHAPTER SIXTEEN

Ydana was torn between following the machine and staying where she was. If she tried to fly ahead to the island to warn the other manticores, she ran the risk of being seen. If she tried to sabotage the flying machine, she ran an even bigger risk. Smashing the wings of such a large contraption would not be as simple as it was with the two-seater one she had encountered before.

No sooner had she even considered such a thing, than a soft roar sounded, so quiet that she almost didn't hear it. Two silhouettes flew towards the flying machine, one headed eagerly in its direction while the other hung back. Ydana recognized the first one as Val, gliding to the top of the balloon.

She heard the sound of something being shot, which made her swoop downwards automatically. But the shot wasn't meant for her. Val's body went limp, and she fell from the sky. Ydana prepared herself to fly to the rescue, but before she could, a large net emerged from the machine, catching Val. Still shocked, Ydana finally darted forward.

Only moments passed before Val woke up and spotted her, and let out a roar. Despite her limited understanding of the way manticores talked to each other, she knew that she was telling her to stay away. When Ydana shook her head, Val roared more insistently.

Val wasn't even showing sadness in her eyes, narrowing them in anger instead. If Ydana so much as moved towards her, thinking that she could chew through the ropes and free her, Val growled again. It was clear to Ydana that Val knew there was nothing she could do but get caught, so she swooped downward, out of the line of sight of the flying machine.

She noticed Tara hovering a ways behind the machine, and flew to join her. She didn't need to be told that they needed to fly ahead to the island and warn the other manticores. Putting enough distance between themselves and the machine that they would not be seen, Ydana and Tara flew through the dark towards the mountains.

Once Ydana had flown away, Val found herself taking human form against her will. Pulling the arrow from her stomach, she held it up, seeing that it was an ordinary crossbow bolt. But it must have been laced with something that was making her unable to stay in manticore form. It was only then that she noticed that she was being pulled upwards, towards the flying machine.

Escaping would do no good if she couldn't take manticore form and fly away, but she tried to struggle against the ropes anyway. Upon reaching the top, she was pulled up, still in the net, by two men who hauled her to her feet. They were both young men, one Hashemi and the other Grusrecian. The Grusrecian looked very nervous.

"I figured I would run into you sooner or later, Valida, but I never imagined we would meet again before I even got to the island," a woman was saying.

"Mitra?" Val hardly needed to look up to know it was her. When she did, she saw that Mitra's hair was dyed black to cover the red highlights in her hair that marked her as a manticore, and she wore a blue veil that covered just her eyes, matching her pale blue dress. "Are you honestly still trying to blend in with the humans, after all this time?"

"That's what I am," Mitra sneered. "I never stopped being human, no matter what you did."

"But it has been over 50 years, likely closer to 70 by now," Val wrenched her arm away from the Grusrecian boy still holding her. She felt ridiculous enough with the net still over her. "How have you explained the fact that you haven't aged? Your siblings are probably past their prime now."

"It's simple, really. I've taken a different name, and posed as my brother's granddaughter who died as a young child. My family knows the truth. Does yours?"

"Just let me go, Mitra," Val growled. "Leave my kind alone. I'm truly sorry for what happened to you, but I've told you that the very fact that you turned means you would never have been happy with the life you had as a human. Can you honestly tell me you were happy before? That you're still happy living as a human?"

"Do I look happy?" Mitra looked anything but, even though Val couldn't see her eyes behind her veil.

"Of course not, because you're still masquerading as a human. The entire point of turning when you were stung was to have a new life that made you happier. And you still could, if you left with me now."

The other people on board who she could see looked too busy to be listening, but Val still wondered why the two men who had pulled her up weren't reacting at all to this conversation. Did they already know that Mitra was a manticore?

"You're not still in love with me after all this time, are you?" Mitra's voice was laced with ice. "Because it's over between us."

Val couldn't help but roll her eyes. Though she wanted nothing more than to let Mitra know precisely what she thought of her now, and that she had moved on, she thought it best not to give her any clue about Ydana, or Tara. Anything she cared about could be used against her, and she wanted to keep Ydana safe.

"I'm not. Believe me, all I want is to rectify what happened. Come with me, and forget about all of this," she tried to yank the rope net over her head, but the Hashemi man still gripping her arm tightened his hold. The longer she stood there with a net over her, the more ridiculous she felt.

"And lose the prestige that comes with being a princess of Hashem? I don't think so."

"You will lose that eventually. Or did you plan to pose as the niece or daughter of relative after relative as you continue to outlive generation after generation? Wouldn't you rather be with people with a similar lifespan to yours?" Val didn't intend for every word she uttered to be dripping in contempt and sarcasm, but they simply would not leave her mouth any other way. Beside her, the Grusrecian boy stiffened at Val's last statement, and because he was no longer holding Val, he shifted his feet, unsure of whether to stand next to Val or Mitra.

Unnerved by the way Mitra stared in silence, Val tried once more to remove the rope net that still covered her.

"Ashar, Sasha, will you help her remove that ridiculous netting?" Mitra turned away. "She won't get away any time soon."

The Hashemi man who still gripped her arm, who she supposed was Ashar, finally let go and threw the last of the netting over Val's head, at the same time as the Grusrecian, Sasha, tied a rope around her wrists so quickly that Val hardly noticed until her hands were tied behind her back.

"And why won't I?" Val asked. "What did you shoot me with?"

"Just because manticores heal quickly doesn't mean there are certain things more dangerous to manticores than to humans. You have reverted to human form because your manticore body knew you would suffer ill effects in that form. Get used to being human, Val, because you'll be that way for awhile."

Val may have been stuck on that ship, but at the very least, she was glad to see the back of Mitra as she left her.

## CHAPTER SEVENTEEN

Though the flying machine was slower than the manticores and could not have kept up with them, Ydana was relieved when they reached the cloudy sky surrounding the mountains. The snow and thick mist would conceal them even if the machine managed to catch up. Opening her mouth as best she could while holding the dead deer once more, Ydana breathed in the snowy air.

She ached to talk to Tara about what had happened, but the mountain range was too cold of an area for taking human form, or even half-human form, for even a moment. It wasn't until they were flying upwards, and the mountain was becoming visible through the mist, that Tara took her half-human form.

"I'm going to spread the word about the manticore hunters!" Tara shouted, her voice nearly getting lost in the wind. "I need you to go to the Ruling Lady and tell her what's happening!"

Feeling the need to argue, Ydana wished she could take half-human form. She highly doubted that she was the best person to go to the Ruling Lady with what had just happened.

"I know what you're thinking," Tara continued to shout against the wind. "But the Ruling Lady doesn't like me at all and may not even know who I am. She *will* remember *you*, and you have more credibility as Val's partner. It has to be you."

Ydana wanted to groan, but she knew Tara was right. The only thing more inconvenient than Ydana, an insignificant human-turned-manticore, showing up in the Ruling Lady's domain, was Tara, who was all of those things but who was merely Val's best friend and not romantic partner.

As soon as they reached the island, Tara dove down with a loud roar, towards the boulder. Despite the lack of sunlight, the boulder was still the gathering spot for many manticores, all of whom looked up at the sound of Tara's roar of warning. The manticores in the sky were also diving down, one by one, to hear what Tara had to say.

Continuing over the forest, Ydana tried to remember the best she could where the Ruling Lady's domain exactly was. She was relieved when she easily found the place she had dove down through with Val and her parents, and from there, flew as quickly as she could through the trees.

As usual, two bat-winged manticores were guarding the entrance to the Ruling Lady's cave. Ydana wasted no time in dropping the dead deer at the entrance, taking her human form, and running up to meet them.

"Valida has been captured by manticore hunters in a flying machine," Ydana began. "A big one. And they're on their way here. It can't be good. We have to tell the Ruling Lady."

The two manticores stared at one another. One of them looked eerily calm, while the other took her human form immediately. Ydana was surprised to see that the guard was Soheila.

"Where is Valida?" Soheila clutched Ydana's shoulders and stared into her eyes as the other guard simply flew away.

"On the flying machine that's headed here. Tara and I saw them capture her, but Val wouldn't let us save her. Tara is warning everyone right now."

Before Ydana finished her sentence, Soheila was already headed into the Ruling Lady's cave. Ydana was not sure if she should follow, but only hesitated a moment before heading inside.

On her throne, the Ruling Lady looked down the staircase at her daughter, Soheila. Her gaze unnerved Ydana, even though it was Soheila she was looking at, not her.

"What is it?" the Ruling Lady spat. "I can tell something has happened. Out with it."

"Manticore hunters are on their way here," Soheila said. Ydana could have applauded her for speaking at all, let alone as calmly as she did. "They have my daughter."

"Bring me a spear!" she barked at the guard next to her before Soheila had even finished.

As soon as the guard handed her a spear, she stood up, spread her wings, and glided down to the ground before rushing out the door, past Ydana. Soheila followed, as did the guard who had stood next to the throne. Not knowing what else to do, Ydana took her manticore form and ran after them.

Ahead of Ydana, Soheila and the Ruling Lady burst upwards through the tops of the trees and began calling to the other manticores they saw in the sky. By the time they reached the boulder, a whole group of manticores was following them. Ydana heard some of them, in half-human form, asking each other what had happened.

As they landed on the boulder, Tara and the other manticores there looked surprised. Clearly, this was the first time many of them had seen the Ruling Lady in a long time. Ydana supposed that few manticores, especially those who were once human, had the occasion to see their ruler more than once.

"Manticore hunters are on their way here," the Ruling Lady thrust the end of her spear into the ground. "They would not be coming here if they weren't armed. We have to be ready for them."

Any manticore in human or half-human form gasped. One manticore standing near Ydana opened her mouth to ask a question, but immediately closed it when the Ruling Lady held a hand up.

"Nobody knows how they found us, but that is not important," the Ruling Lady did not put her hand down. "All that matters is that we make sure they leave, and never come back. Everyone will immediately disperse themselves to all sides of the island and find crevices to hide in. Whichever side the manticore hunters arrive on will begin fighting them, while the rest of you, who will still be hidden, will come around and cut off the manticore hunters' escape. These people have a rather large flying machine, and they likely have weapons aboard, so be prepared. I will be on the south side of the island, where the manticore hunters are most likely to arrive."

"And where should I go, mother?" Soheila asked as the Ruling Lady turned to go.

"Choose a few people to help you rescue Valida," the Ruling Lady lowered her voice. "I don't imagine you would be able to concentrate on anything else."

Ydana worried about the way that the Ruling Lady was deliberately keeping Val's capture a secret. Though it could worry the rest of the manticores unnecessarily if they knew, it could also endanger Val's life if too few people knew she was aboard the flying machine.

Once the Ruling Lady flew away, and the rest of the manticores leapt up into the sky, one by one, Ydana saw that Soheila was beckoning her closer.

"Come with me to rescue Valida." It was not a question.

Ydana nodded.

"What will happen to Val?" Tara joined them.

"The Ruling Lady has given us permission to rescue her," Soheila explained. "Both of you go to my daughter's house and find weapons, while I find my husband. Meet me at my dwelling."

Though Ydana hardly knew what she would do with a weapon, being unable to take half-human form, she followed Tara.

Val's house was only a short distance away from the boulder, and Tara and Ydana flew straight to the upper floor where the weapons were kept.

"A bow won't be much use if we're going aboard the flying machine, but it may come in handy before that," Tara packed several arrows into a quiver before slinging it, and a bow, over her shoulder. "More likely I'll need a knife."

Having seen Tara practice shooting in the woods before, Ydana knew she was a good shot and would be the best person to use Val's bow.

"What can I do?" Ydana took her human form. "I can't transform…"

"You'll at least need a knife when you get on board the flying machine," Tara handed her one of Val's knives from the shelf.

It was a small knife on a string. Putting it around her neck by the string, Ydana practiced unsheathing the knife a few times.

"Leave it to Val to have no armor," Tara groaned. "Maybe Soheila has an extra set. Armor for manticores has to be very light, or else we can't fly. Unfortunately, wings are the biggest target, and it's hard to put any armor on our wings. Not that we usually get attacked like this, but it's good to have."

Ydana could see why, as a manticore's body was already very heavy for their wings. A manticore's wingspan was much longer in proportion to their bodies than that of a bird, to account for the extra weight, but Ydana couldn't imagine adding the weight of armor.

"I suppose I will be doing without, in the hopes that I don't get attacked," Ydana sighed.

It was not long before Ydana and Tara were hiding in one of the crevices on the side of the island, with Val's parents. Soheila and Vash were in half-human form, wearing manticore armor that covered their torsos, and clutching spears. Next to them, Tara fiddled with the buckles on her own borrowed gauntlets.

Ydana, armorless and still in Manticore form, felt foolish as she plastered herself against the wall of dirt. It felt like too much time was passing by as they waited, almost in silence, though it had barely been long enough to get hungry or thirsty.

When the soft whirring sound that Ydana recognized from the flying machine sounded in the distance, her ears perked up.

"Let's go," Soheila whispered.

"Remember, you go ahead of me," Vash said to Ydana, "Just fly towards the machine as quickly as you can. If they have any of the small flying machines and come after us, I will deal with them. Tara, you stay back and shoot anyone you see getting close to us."

Ydana nodded her understanding, but her stomach felt as if it were flipping over. She wished she were able to take half-human form and shoot arrows as well as Tara did so that she could stay out of the way, but she knew that she was needed on the flying machine, to help rescue Val. Hopefully no harm had come to her already.

The beating of many sets of manticore wings outside was their cue to fly out into the open. Staring, openmouthed, Ydana took in the sight of nearly 100 manticores swarming around. She had never seen this many of them in the sky at once.

As soon as her eyes traveled to the flying machine, she took off towards it, followed by Vash and Soheila. The manticore hunters clearly had not expected to be met with such immediate resistance, and were only now opening up a landing dock of their flying machine to allow the one- and two-seaters out to fight the manticores. Only when Ydana came very close did one come after her, and she noticed that it was quick to crumble to the ground. She supposed that one of Tara's arrows had hit its mark.

She raced up to the flying machine and only briefly glanced around for an opening of some kind before seeing that Val's cousins Vaja and Dara were bashing their spears into the window in the hopes of cracking it open. Another manticore was jumping onto the front window, surprising the pilots. A glance up showed several manticores landing on the roof and sides of the balloon and poking it with their spears repeatedly. The balloon would not be popped so easily, however.

Vaja and Dara finally made a large enough crack in the window and broke through, clearing the sharp pieces away. Vaja grasped the edge, took human form, and hauled herself through the small space before returning to half-human form on the inside. Ydana saw her drawing a sword from a scabbard on her back and doing battle with the people inside. Soon after, Dara joined her and was on the inside, stabbing one of the manticore hunters in the stomach with a spear.

Before Ydana could join them, a rope caught Soheila around the neck, the other end of which was held by someone in one of the small flying machines. Leaping for the rope, Ydana took human form and grasped the rope. Not daring to look down, she unsheathed the knife that hung around her neck. With only a few quick cuts, the rope was severed. As Vash tore through the sky and began tearing the small flying machine's wings apart with his spear, Ydana began falling from the sky.

Before Ydana could take her manticore form once more, Soheila grasped her at the wrist and lifted her to the window. Hauling herself through, she took in her surroundings. The two manticores who had just started doing battle inside of the machine were already laying on the ground in human form, bleeding. The spear that Dara had been using was lodged into the stomach of a now dead manticore hunter.

Turning back towards the window, she undid the latch that held the door closed, allowing Vash and Soheila to swoop in past her, wings outstretched. No sooner had they landed, than Soheila bent her wing, wincing in pain. Ydana looked past Soheila to see three manticore hunters standing in the stairwell. One, a Hashemi man, was clutching his arm, blood seeping through the fabric of his sleeve. In front of him, a Hashemi woman with a strange veil over her eyes held a crossbow.

Vash wasted no time in leaping at them, taking his fully manticore form. As Soheila took her human form, Ydana wondered why she had done that instead of attack. When Vash also took his human form as soon as he tackled the woman, and was dragged to his feet by the two male manticore hunters, Ydana realized that the transformation couldn't have been done willingly.

A shudder ran through her, and she backed up towards the window again. She looked out the window to see if there were any other manticores she could signal to help, but what she saw shook her to the core. The island was already farther away than it had been when she had entered the flying machine, and it was rapidly being consumed by fire.

## CHAPTER EIGHTEEN

All of the manticores Ydana saw outside were flying frantically, pouring water from the river to quell the flames. A couple of them even fetched snow from the mountain below, to throw down onto the fire. But she noticed that no one dared to get too close to the fire.

Vash still tried to attack the three manticore hunters, even in the human form he had been forced, somehow, to revert to, while Soheila ran forward to join him, giving Ydana a look that told her to stay put. But Vash was quickly apprehended by one of the manticore hunters.

Ydana hardly had time to be shocked as Soheila, spear in hand, charged at the female manticore hunter, who, without so much as blinking, drew a sword from the scabbard at her waist and stabbed Soheila straight through the stomach. Eyes narrowed in fury, Soheila ripped the sword out of her own body and stabbed her opponent right back.

When Ydana didn't think anything could be more surprising, the woman gripped Soheila's throat in her hand, digging her nails into Soheila's flesh. She looked completely unfazed by the sword through her stomach. Vash, still in the clutches of one of the other manticore hunters, thrashed against his captor's grip and called Soheila's name.

"Take them all below," the veiled woman croaked as she and Soheila both dropped to the ground.

Though Ydana knew that Soheila, Dara and Vaja were not dead, for a mere weapon could not kill a manticore, the sight of Soheila dropping to the ground was still shocking. Putting a hand to her mouth, she fought to stifle the choking sobs that threatened to escape. With her other hand, she tightened her grip on the knife.

"Your highness!" a familiar voice shouted.

Ydana could hardly believe who she was seeing kneel beside the woman, whose veil had slipped but whose face Ydana still could not see from that distance. Gathering her into his arms was Sasha.

Everything Tara saw was chaos. Nearly 100 manticores were doing all they could to contain the fire, but all it did was spread. Soon, the focus shifted from attempting to put the fire out, to getting everyone to a safe place.

She supposed that starting a fire and burning the island to a crisp had been the manticore hunters' plan all along. That was why they had left as soon as the fire had started, and why they had been willing to sacrifice so many of their own for a battle that humans could hardly win.

During the battle, Tara had finally been attacked by one of the flying machines, which must have seen that she was the one shooting them all down. To her horror, they had had a harpoon ready to launch at her. It had been the Ruling Lady herself who had jumped in between them, taking the blow herself. Tara had had little time to wonder why her leader was risking her life for someone as insignificant as herself, and had instead been horrified at the way the Ruling Lady's body had simply dangled there by a rope attached to the harpoon through her side. Taking manticore form, the Ruling Lady had roared at Tara to get away. Flying away as quickly as she could, Tara had caught a glimpse of several other manticores coming to the Ruling Lady's aid, cutting at the rope and catching her when she fell. Tara had not seen the Ruling Lady after that.

Fire Consumes Us

Shaking her head in an attempt to rid herself of the memory, Tara turned her focus back to the fire. On the ground below her, a cub too young to fly was attempting to outrun the flames. Not thinking, Tara took her manticore form and dove down, swooping him up in her mouth by the scruff. In the sky once more, she looked down to see another manticore get too close to the fire before taking human form automatically and practically disintegrating in front of her eyes. Not wanting to shock the cub with such a sight, if he hadn't fainted already, she turned away and flew towards the lake.

The area around the lake had not caught fire, but manticores were swimming to the middle anyway, not wanting to risk it. Some sat atop the rocks in the middle of the lake, taking human form so as to make room for others, while other manticores brought rafts and logs to float on in case they grew too tired to tread water. A few even stayed ashore, prepared to dive into the water if the fire came too close. One father sat just ashore, in half-human form, preparing to push the raft that housed his two cubs towards the middle of the lake if he had to. The cubs, just like the one in Tara's care, had batlike wings, because they had, of course, been manticores since birth.

Recognizing Tara, the father motioned her over, still holding onto the raft.

"Where are his parents?" he asked as Tara placed the cub into the raft beside the others. He knew that Tara had no cubs of her own and that this one couldn't be hers.

Groups of manticores continued to dive in to fill vases and jars with water, before leaving again in an attempt to control the fire. Looking sadly up towards the flames that rose up into the dark sky, Tara shook the ash out of her mane.

"I don't know whose cub he is," Tara admitted once she returned to half-human form. "I just saved him from the fire."

Though the cub was not old enough to take human form and give her the names of his parents, Tara was certain that he would know them if he saw them.

Flying over the lake, Tara soon saw the Ruling Lady, in human form, laying on a raft, one of her guards on either side. She sighed in relief, seeing that the Ruling Lady had made it away from the fire despite her wounds, which, evidently, had not yet healed. Tara wondered why that was, as several hours had passed, and manticores usually healed themselves in that amount of time.

Tara landed in the water as softly as she could, and swam to the Ruling Lady and her guards.

"What's happened?" she whispered. "Why isn't her majesty healed?"

"What business is it of yours, girl?" the guard closest to her barked.

"Leave the girl alone," the Ruling Lady said in a voice that was very strong for one wounded. "She hasn't done anything wrong."

Hesitantly, Tara bent over the raft.

"Honestly, child, you don't need to be so far away," the Ruling Lady whispered.

"What's happened?" Tara bent closer. "Why hasn't your wound healed?"

"Manticore hunters' weapons have had something…wrong with them for many years now. Whether we are shot or stabbed with most any of their weapons, we revert back to human form within minutes, and have a difficult time regaining our true forms."

Tara thought back to the way Val had been shot when she had last seen her. Had she been forced to take human form after that?

"Whatever they have done to these weapons," the Ruling Lady continued, "it's something a manticore can't process, so it makes us remain in human form. Hopefully temporarily."

In that moment, Tara ached for the Ruling Lady, and for Val. What if they were unable to take manticore form ever again? She shuddered, thinking of how soon she would need to face the manticore hunters again. Would she, too, be shot, and possibly never fly again?

"Why did you save me?" Tara held the Ruling Lady's hand. "You are far more valuable than I am, so why save me?"

"Am I? I'm not so sure about that. I would happily risk myself for any of my people, but a youngling like you most of all. Even if you were not my granddaughter's friend."

"Why?" Tara had always thought that Val's grandmother had forgotten she existed, or perhaps even disliked her.

"Because you are capable of so much more than I. Now go and follow the manticore hunters back to their hole. Find out where they went."

Tara began to shake her head, then thought better of it. "Of course. But you can't stay here. The manticore hunters may come back to finish us off."

"We will not be here long. But if we are not, we will be split up and some of us will be hidden in the mountains below. Find them, and they will tell the rest of us. We will eradicate the humans responsible, and make sure that not another manticore hunter breathes this air again. Go!"

"I will save Valida, I promise."

Turning away from the crowd, Tara took her manticore form and flapped her large wings, launching herself into the air. She flew away from the island as quickly as possible, so as not to be tempted to turn back and see her home burning.

Fire Consumes Us

## CHAPTER NINETEEN

Ydana held on to the outside of the flying machine, crouched low underneath the window, and occasionally peeked inside to see if anyone was there. She was tempted to take her manticore form, to stave off the cold, but she knew that that would only make her more likely to be seen.

Finally, after what felt like hours had passed, Sasha appeared, and he was by himself. Standing up, Ydana watched him grow wide-eyed when he saw her.

"What are you doing here?" he whispered and glanced over his shoulder to make sure no one else was approaching.

"What am I doing here? What about you?" Ydana allowed him to help her through the window. "The last time I saw you, you were no manticore hunter."

"Things change," Sasha gripped her arm and finished helping her through the window. "In fact, last I heard, you were still at boarding school. I'm awfully glad you're not, but do you realize how close to danger you just came?"

"I saw that burning island with my own eyes, Sasha. Of course I know. In fact, people I know may be dead right now."

"Very few things can kill a manticore. But I don't want you to meet the same fate that your friends did on this ship. You should get to safety."

"Never. I came here to see them." Ydana had very nearly said 'save them', but caught herself just in time. She certainly did not need Sasha changing his mind about helping her. If he was a manticore hunter now, she couldn't know what else had changed. "Where are they?"

Holding a finger to his lips, Sasha motioned for her to follow him. He opened a door that she had not known was there, and they descended the stairs.

It did not take long to reach the bottom, as the flying machine was not especially large. Once there, Ydana caught sight of a large cage with five figures sitting in it. The only light in the cell came from five candles, which were tied between each of their wrists.

"Ydana?" Val turned towards her.

"Val, are you alright?" she knelt beside her, with the bars between them. "Why do you all have candles tied to you?"

"You don't know, do you?" Val whispered. "A manticore's weakness is fire. Being this close to it makes us stay in human form."

"But…what about the fire at your parents' house?" Ydana looked from Val to his parents. "You sat next to it while in manticore form."

"Yes, we are able to sit by small cooking fires," Soheila explained, "but we aren't as close to them, usually, as we are to these candles here."

"But they already shot you with their special weapons," Ydana pointed out. "That turned you all to human form, so why do they need those candles?"

"It must only last so long," Soheila spoke up. "I'm not sure what makes their weapons special that way, but perhaps their effect does not last long enough for them to ensure that we won't escape during the flight."

"Where are they taking you?" Ydana asked, but was only met with blank stares from Val, Soheila, Vash, Vaja and Dara. Instead, she turned to look at Sasha, who shook his head. She was unsure of whether he didn't know where they were going or was simply not allowed to reveal such a thing.

"'You'? What's happening to *you*, Ydana?" Val had clearly not missed the way she had not included herself in her statement. "They aren't taking you someplace worse, are they?"

"I haven't been shot with whatever they gave you," Ydana lowered her voice. "They haven't seen me yet."

"Oh? Then why did he bring you here?" Val looked past her at Sasha.

"He's an old friend."

"You're friends with a manticore hunter?" Vaja said, angrily.

"He wasn't a manticore hunter before. Listen, I'm just trying to find out how to help you."

Vaja was about to say something else, but Vash silenced her with a glance.

"Ydana, listen to me," Vash turned to her. "We are working out a plan. It is best if you escape while you have the chance, and go back to warn the others."

"The whole island was in flames," Ydana felt the pressure of tears spring to her eyes. "I'm sure everyone who survived is gone from there now."

"You still need to get out," Val looked at her with concern in her eyes. "Please. I'd hate for anything to happen to you. That veiled woman...you saw her, didn't you? You had to."

Ydana nodded.

"That's Mitra."

"What?" Ydana covered her mouth. "But you said she..."

She suddenly remembered the way that the veiled woman had seemed to die, before waking up again. Ydana should have known, especially with the way the woman kept her eyes covered.

"I'm afraid it's true," Sasha said from behind her. She had nearly forgotten that he was present.

"So, the reason the manticore hunters hate us so much is because of her?" Ydana asked.

"No," Vash spoke up again. "Their hatred of us started long before she came along."

A look of dread crossed Sohelia's face as if she realized what he was about to say.

"One day, hundreds of years ago, a Hashemi prince was turned into a manticore," Vash lowered his voice to a whisper, looking over Ydana's shoulder at Sasha to make sure he didn't hear. "It was a horrible scandal throughout the country, despite his parents' efforts to keep it quiet. They disinherited him as soon as it happened, and their younger son became the heir in his place. By age three, the prince who was now a manticore was locked away, seen by nobody, and received no love from his parents. He ran away before he had even turned, and no one ever came looking for him. He took jobs in the field and in the mines, anything he could get, and slept in a closet until the day he finally turned."

Ydana felt for the young prince-turned-manticore. She couldn't imagine being out in the streets the way he was. Her own parents may have been upset with her, but at least they still cared about her.

"Unfortunately," Vash continued, "the younger prince, who had been made heir in his place, died very young, and the Podishah had no other children. Members of his family became manticore hunters to bring the true prince home, while rival families became manticore hunters to get rid of the prince before he could reemerge. One such manticore hunter took over the kingdom when the Podishah died with no heir, and stopped trying to bring the prince home, urging his family members to begin hunting manticores to kill them instead. Manticore hunting continued to spread, as the rival families encouraged as many people to take up the trade as possible. Anything to increase the odds of the true prince coming back. I doubt any of them remember that that is why it all started, but they continue to hunt our kind."

"Do you think...could he still be out there somewhere?" Ydana wondered. "He must have found the manticore who stung him, and made friends, and found a new family instead of the people who shunned him like that."

"I guarantee he did," Vash smiled at Soheila.

"Wait..." Val looked at her parents, confused. "That can't be. The Prince was you?"

Her parents nodded. Vaja and Dara looked equally confused.

"I am hoping that we can take back the throne and make Hashem a place where humans and manticores can all live in peace," Vash said. "But a lot of people are going to stand in our way, so we need to be prepared. Not just now, but in years to come."

"I hope you're ready for the battle ahead," Soheila looked at Val, her face not betraying any nervousness. "Ydana, you should leave while you can, and..."

"She should stay here," Vash interrupted. "If she leaves, the manticore hunters will know where she went."

"It's just me," Sasha spoke for the first time in a while. "I'm the only one who knows she's here."

"You don't know that," Vash glared at him. "How much do you trust Mitra, anyway?"

Sasha looked at the ground, nervously. "Her name is Sahar now."

"You're right," Soheila looked at Vash, "Ydana should stay here. But not in the same room, or else she will be caught the same way we are."

"You, manticore hunter, can we trust you to find the best hiding place for Ydana?" Val glared at Sasha.

"Of course you can. Ydana is my friend," Sasha said. "Believe me, I'm not a manticore hunter because I hate you. In fact, I only learned recently that hunting manticores was the family business. I'm only here because my parents insisted on it."

"But that doesn't mean they haven't convinced you in the meantime," Val glanced down at the candle tied between the ropes that tied her hands together, looking as if she wanted to tear it up. "We still don't know that we can trust you."

"Do you have a choice?" Sasha asked. "Listen, I loved Ydana before she left. Something like that doesn't just die."

"Now I like you even less," Val growled. "You had better keep her safe, or else I'll..."

"Valida," Soheila interrupted him.

"I'll be fine, Val," Ydana wished she could hold her hand through the bars.

"Here, just get into this closet," Sasha went to a door at the end of the room and, finding it unlocked, opened it. "Stay in there, and no one will suspect you."

Glancing back at Val one last time, Ydana got into the small closet and allowed Sasha to close the door on her.

Fire Consumes Us

Sitting on the cold ground, Ydana hugged her knees. She hated that Val and her parents were in the same room and yet she couldn't even see them. Despite the turmoil in her mind, she dozed off. It was impossible to say how long, and when she woke, she wondered if the flying machine had already landed and her companions had already been herded off. But she dared not open the door to peek outside, just in case.

Finally, when she was growing hungry and thirsty, voices sounded from outside of her closet.

"They're tied up, what can they possibly do to you?" said a woman's voice, it had to be Mitra. "Just prick them and be done with it."

Ydana shivered. They were dosing them with whatever was keeping them in human form, yet again. The thought of anyone hurting Val made her blood boil, but she would only be caught herself if she tried to fight them. She did not even know how many of them there were.

"Don't you know anything, Sasha?" Mitra scolded again. "If you don't shape up before we're married, I'll be marrying a coward! How do you think that will look?"

Married? Ydana was shocked. She couldn't imagine her friend, who had loved *her*, being engaged to someone as terrible as Mitra was supposed to be. Perhaps Sasha really did do everything his parents told him to, and any interest he used to have in her before she turned was only to win his parents' approval.

Though she had known for some time that her relationship with Val went far beyond the feelings she had had for Sasha, she had still wondered how things would have played out with Sasha. But now she knew. If Sasha's parents were manticore hunters as well, as indicated by Sasha's comment about "the family business" earlier, then they were only allowing him to court her in order to use her for something. At a snap of his father's fingers, Sasha had looked elsewhere for a suitable match, and that would still have happened later, had their relationship progressed.

She was startled from her thoughts when another man's voice sounded, from much closer to her door.

"The only other vial is in here."

"No," came Sasha's voice. "I moved it. I didn't think we'd have any manticore prisoners, so I took it upstairs where we would remember to take it back with us."

Panicked, Ydana looked around her for something, anything, that could allow her to hide. But all she found were a few tiny boxes on the shelf above her. Not even a stray piece of cloth she could lay under. She braced herself as the door opened.

## CHAPTER TWENTY

As soon as the door opened, Ydana took her manticore form and leaped out, onto the Hashemi man who had opened it. In front of her, Mitra was also taking manticore form, shaking her mane and roaring loudly in Ydana's direction. Ydana did not wait. She pounced on Mitra, who leaped out of the way just in time, but not before Ydana bit her in the leg.

Behind Mitra, another Hashemi manticore hunter gripped Val's arm and was leading her out of the cage, still tied but without a candle tied in between the ropes. Ydana didn't think. She darted past Mitra the moment she had a chance. Before she knew it, she was reaching out towards Val with human arms, while still running on four manticore legs.

It was only after she gripped Val around the waist and hoisted her into her arms, that she realized she had taken half-human form for the first time. She had little time to celebrate, as she heard the commotion behind her, of manticore hunters running after her.

As soon as she reached the top of the stairs, she felt a terrible pain in the back of her shoulder. It wasn't so much the pain that bothered her, as what it spelled: her doom. As soon as she felt it, she somehow knew there was no escaping. Dropping Val, she crumpled down the stairs and hit the ground with a thud, fully human.

Clutching her shoulder, Ydana directed her gaze back up towards the top of the staircase. With a roar that tore from her lungs, she signaled for Val to keep running. But Val only made it a few more steps with her arms and legs tied, before one of the two Hashemi manticore hunters caught up with her easily.

The man punched Val in the face so hard that Ydana winced at the sound. Val slumped down to lay on the stairs, motionless. Ydana wanted to cover her mouth, but knew that doing so would make her appear weak. Instead, she turned to face Mitra, her eyes burning.

"It would appear we had a stowaway," Mitra, back in human form, stood over her, looking around at the other manticore hunters. "Did any of you know about this?"

They shook their heads.

"You didn't honestly think that pathetic attempt at escaping would succeed, did you?" Mitra finally looked down at Ydana. Her veil was askew, and her bright manticore eyes glowed in the darkness.

Ydana narrowed her eyes at the hateful woman. She would not answer her. Close by, one of the Hashemi men was trying to contain Soheila, and finally knocked her unconscious with a blow to the face. Vash roared from inside of the cage. Looking at Soheila's unconscious form, now in the arms of the manticore hunter, Ydana guessed that she had attempted to stop some of the manticore hunters from running after Ydana and Val.

Behind Mitra, Sasha gave Ydana a worried look.

"Isn't this girl your friend, Sasha?" Mitra didn't take her eyes off of Ydana. "I could swear she's the same girl from the party."

Sasha gulped. "Yes, your highness. I do know her. It has been some time since…"

"Are you sure you aren't covering up for her? You didn't exactly jump to stop her from running away. And look, there is the vial that you said you moved."

Sasha opened his mouth to protest, but was interrupted again by Mitra.

"You had better have a good explanation. Get to work."

Ydana was surprised that Mitra didn't actually demand an explanation from Sasha, but perhaps there was only so much Mitra wanted to belittle him in front of the other manticore hunters.

She struggled against the manticore hunter who pulled her to her feet. He was quickly joined by the one who had knocked Val unconscious. It pained her to see Sasha pouring whatever was in the vial onto the knife he took from his belt. Entering the cage, he paused and looked around nervously.

She thought, for a moment, that he was only pretending to carry out his task, but when Vash betrayed the slightest of pained expressions, she knew that Sasha had truly used the knife on him. Once he had done the same to Vaja and Dara, he put out the candles and untied them from each of their ropes before pulling Vash to his feet and leading him from the cage.

Vash and Dara were made to carry Val and Soheila, who were still unconscious. The manticores followed Mitra and her manticore hunters up the stairs. It was then that Ydana realized that her companions' ankles were tied just loosely enough to allow them to painstakingly ascend the stairs, but not enough for them to run anywhere. Sasha and one of the Hashemi brought up the rear, their crossbows trained on the manticores.

Once they descended the ramp from the flying machine, Ydana knew where they were. In the predawn light, the palace courtyard looked slightly different from what she remembered, as it had been several years since she had last seen it.

If only she could take manticore form for only a moment, she could fly up the walls and easily make it to her parents' house from there, even on foot. Surely if they knew who the manticore hunters were in the royal family, and in Sasha's family, they could do something to help. Otherwise, no one would know who the manticore hunters were, for she and her companions were surely dead otherwise. She concentrated on her transformation, but could not seem to take manticore form no matter how hard she tried.

Looking around, she spotted a thick vine. Perhaps it was thick enough to hold her weight, if she climbed fast enough. Doing her best to look depressed, she looked from Val's unconscious form, in her father's arms, to the ground.

"I know what you're thinking," Vash whispered. "Don't. You'll…"

"Stop talking!" the Hashemi with the weapon barked from behind them.

Why didn't Vash think she should escape? Was it because she could get lost? Perhaps he did not know how close her house was to the palace. Or perhaps there was another reason. She took a deep breath. If she did not get out and warn someone, they were all dead anyway. She had nothing to lose.

Once they passed by the wall with the vine she had spotted, Ydana didn't dare hesitate. She bolted. Though her hands were tied, and her shoulder still ached horribly where she had been shot, her feet had not been tied.

A crossbow bolt flew past her. She ran diagonally, as unpredictably as possible. It was difficult to run with her wrists tied together in front of her, and she found herself stumbling, but she continued to run. She had to make it out. Just when she suspected that it was Sasha shooting, and missing on purpose, she felt the back of her arm sting. Despite the pain, she continued running. Wounds such as this may kill a human, but not a manticore.

As she approached the vine, she jumped up and gripped it with her hands, walking her legs up as high as she could go. As she was about to reach the top, she saw a knife sail over her head to embed itself in the vine near the top. Before she could climb up any higher, the vine snapped where the knife had cut it. As she fell backwards to the ground, she caught a glimpse of a manticore flying through the sky, high above her.

## CHAPTER TWENTY-ONE

Having fully expected to hit the ground, Ydana was surprised to instead be caught in someone's arms.

"You had better not try that again," Sasha whispered in her ear. "Princess Sahar will definitely want you punished now."

"I had to try," Ydana's voice cracked with soreness.

"I know."

No sooner had Ydana gotten to her feet and turned to face the group once more, than Mitra took her manticore form and charged her. In moments, Ydana was swept up into Mitra's jaws, her sharp teeth poking straight through her stomach and in between her ribs. If Ydana were human, she surely would have been dead in an instant. But because she wasn't, Mitra was clearly trying to torture her.

The world blurred past as Mitra ran into the palace, still carrying Ydana, before throwing her to the ground somewhere inside.

"Your majesty, I have set fire to the manticores' floating island," Mitra took her human form once more, not bothering to arrange her veil so that it covered her eyes. Everyone nearby must know she was a manticore anyway. "We have six prisoners, including the one who stung me."

Ydana struggled to sit up, finding that she couldn't move. The wound behind her shoulder was only finally starting to heal, but the wounds from Mitra's teeth showed no sign of lessening. Whatever the manticore hunters' weapons had been coated with must have also slowed down the manticores' healing abilities. She had never felt so vulnerable.

"Well done, Mitra," came the Podishah's voice. Ydana could not move her head to see what he looked like.

"I only ask permission that I exact the revenge that I want to on the manticore who stung me," Mitra continued. "You can do what you want with the rest of the prisoners."

This was it. Ydana felt as if her fate were sealed. There was nothing else she could do to get away, to warn anyone. Tears threatened to spill from her eyes.

She was dimly aware of her companions being led inside.

"Ydana," Val gasped her name as she stumbled to kneel beside her, her hands still tied. "What did you do to her, Mitra?"

Her voice sounded as defeated as Ydana felt, though she may have been downplaying how upset she was so that Mitra wouldn't know what Ydana meant to her.

"I'm fine, Val…ida," Ydana whispered, adding her full name as an afterthought, to avoid betraying familiarity and giving Mitra a reason to torture her further.

"Take these vermin to the dungeon," came the Podishah's voice again.

As one of the manticore hunters bent to help Ydana up, Val dropped to all fours in front of her and growled. All of the manticores except for Mitra seemed to take a step back from her. Ydana wasn't sure how Val was able to pick her up and stand while her feet were tied, but she somehow did. After that, Ydana dropped in and out of consciousness as they were led to the dungeon.

"You should…run," Ydana's voice came out in a croak, and she wasn't even sure Val had heard her. "Save yourself."

"Not while you're like this," she whispered back. "Besides, I wouldn't make it two steps before I'd be caught again."

The six manticores were made to go into a cage that looked similar to the one on the flying machine, only once the door was closed behind them, it erupted in flames. Ydana didn't see what the manticore hunters did to make that happen, but she guessed that it was coated in a flammable substance of some sort. Clearly, the manticore hunters had thought of everything.

Setting Ydana down, Val untied the rope around her wrist, before turning to allow her father to untie her own. There was no need for candles to keep them from untying their ropes, as there was no escaping a burning cage.

"What are they going to do with us?" Vaja wondered.

"One way or another, I hope to never find out," Soheila said, in a voice that gave Ydana chills.

For the first time, Ydana truly realized that they may not live through the ordeal. Her parents may never find out what happened to her, and Mitra would still be out there to kill other manticores. The very idea of Mitra being the last manticore alive after possibly having killed everyone on the island was enough to make Ydana sick.

Despite the throbbing pain all over her body, Ydana sat up.

"They have to put out this fire at some point in order to let us out, I'm sure," Soheila continued. "At that point, we need to keep them from coming in here to dose us again."

"What is it that they're coating their weapons with?" Ydana asked. "Why can't we transform?"

"It's manticore blood burnt in a fire," said a voice that Ydana felt she had not heard in ages.

"Misty?" she turned her gaze to the bundle of fabric that lay in the corner.

To her surprise, her manticore companion from the Meacham Academy was sitting right before her very eyes, her clothing filthy, her hair a mess, and her arms covered in bandages. She must have been there ever since Ydana last saw her, and she felt guilty for having allowed Misty to be caught, even if there was nothing she could have done save be caught alongside her.

"Believe me, Ydana," Misty continued, "I have tried everything to get away, and yet here I am."

"I'm so sorry," Ydana shook her head, still trying to wrap her mind around how Misty was sitting here with her.

"You know her?" Soheila asked.

"A Grusrecian manticore?" Vaja looked surprised.

"She's the one other manticore from boarding school," Ydana explained. She had mentioned her to Val, Soheila and Vash before. "She was chased away by manticore hunters when she turned, and I never knew if she was able to get away from them or not."

"Yes, I had the misfortune of turning for the first time right in view of the public, and in front of some dreadful girl's fiancée who happened to be a manticore hunter," Misty continued. "Of course, it didn't help that they were starving us."

"They were starving you?" Val looked at Ydana with concern.

"I told you about that," Ydana explained. "We weren't permitted any more meat than I had been at home, and our extra etiquette lessons consisted mostly of ignoring the tasty rabbits that were running around the room. Impossible. And if we failed, we got no supper, which made things worse yet."

"Wow, that must have been terrible," Vaja looked shocked.

"You were saying you know what it is they put on their weapons," Soheila knelt beside Misty.

"It's my blood," Misty said as if it were the most normal thing in the world. "Manticore blood burned in a fire. I'm not sure why that's what works, but it does."

Ydana tried not to let the horror she felt show on her face. Looking at the bandages all over Misty's arms, they must have cut her many times to collect her blood.

"Fire is the only thing that can kill a manticore," Soheila's voice was the most gentle that Ydana had ever heard it. "Something burnt like that must make us turn to human form because our bodies are telling us that we're in less danger in human form. Manticore blood must be the only thing that can make it stay in our system for more than a few moments."

"It must wear off at some point," Dara said. "They already had to give it to us again during the flight here."

"It does, but that's why we're kept in a cage of fire," Misty looked around them at the flaming bars.

"Until we come up with a plan, perhaps we should avoid transforming even if it does wear off," Soheila decided. "That way, if any of the manticore hunters come back, they will see us in human form only and think we're too scared to or unable to transform."

"And we probably shouldn't be heard talking too much, either," Vash added. "If someone comes in, they need to not see us suddenly go quiet as if we're up to something. They need to see us looking as dejected as possible. We should even just take turns sleeping so that they believe it. From now on, we talk only in pairs, and only in whispers. But if someone tries to come in, we transform. And make it sudden."

Everyone nodded.

Ydana did not know how long they sat in the cage. Her wounds were slowly healing, and Val, her head still hurting from when she was knocked unconscious, lay her head in Ydana's lap.

"Is she the one who stung you?" Misty mouthed to Ydana from a few feet away.

Ydana nodded.

"Nice," Misty smiled.

Glad that no one else was witnessing this conversation, Ydana smiled back.

Before long, Mitra and two of her fellow manticore hunters entered. Mitra had her usual veil in place once more when she peeked in on them.

"Now who wants to offer up an arm," she gestured to one of her men, who held out a knife.

Soheila let out a low growl.

"We can't let the same one do it again," the man not holding the knife said. "She's at her limit for now."

It was then that Ydana understood what was happening. They weren't here to dose them with more of the substance. They were here to collect manticore blood from somebody.

"Why are we still alive, Mitra," Val asked, getting up. "You could have killed us back on the island when you burnt everything up, but you didn't."

"If I had, you may have died or you may not have," Mitra said. "I want to make sure, when the time comes, that you die, and that I see it with my own eyes to make absolutely sure you never return."

"Never speak to my daughter that way again," Soheila growled.

"You," Mitra ignored Soheila and pointed to Ydana. "You're already bleeding, so it would be easy."

"You'll have to come in here and get me, then, because getting to my feet is much too difficult in this condition," Ydana surprised herself with how confident she sounded.

"As you wish," Mitra's voice was like ice. Ydana felt a sharp pain in the side of her neck, and put a hand to it. That was the last thing she remembered.

"Father, we have to let the manticores go," Sasha stormed into the room. His father turned towards him, and to Sasha's surprise, so did the Podishah.

"I'm terribly sorry, your majesty," Sasha's father stammered. "The boy doesn't know what he's saying. He has had a long day."

"Yes I do!"

Sasha could say no more as his father rushed him out of the room, gripping him roughly by the shirtsleeve.

"You had better have a good reason for this," his father hardly looked like himself, his eyes narrowed in anger.

"Those manticores down there need to go free," Sasha tried to speak as quickly as he could, before his father could stop him. "One of them is Ydana, and her parents would be…"

"What good is Ydana now that she has turned? You can't honestly still be missing her when you are about to have a much more prestigious marriage. That girl is not worth saving."

"This isn't about my marriage!" Sasha spoke so loudly that his voice echoed around the hallway. "Ydana is worth saving! She is my friend!"

"Manticores cannot be our friends!"

"It's terrible what we're doing. It's hardly any different from their kind killing us. They're people just like…"

"They're NOT people," his father growled. For a moment, Sasha felt compelled to agree simply from how scared he felt. "Do *people* sting innocent children? Do *people* hunt our game, and scare away our tourists?"

"The entire reason Leon was stung by a manticore was because he would never have been happy here!" Sasha said more loudly than he had intended. Even saying his brother's name shocked him, but he saw that it shocked his father even more. That name was hardly ever mentioned in their household, yet this was the second time he had mentioned it since becoming a manticore hunter.

When Sasha finished his sentence, his father did not come up with a retort. Leon was there, in the silence, as he had always been. Sasha's family had gone years at a time without mentioning Leon's name, yet he was always there, in the pauses, in everything that was left unsaid.

Sasha had watched his mother drink herself to sleep countless times to forget the son who had disappeared, while his father grew more vigilant in his hatred of manticores. Soon after Leon had disappeared from boarding school, never to be seen again, Sasha's parents had locks installed on every window, even though they had already been the only house on the block with windows covered in glass, since the day Leon was first stung.

He had always wondered why his family had even stayed in Hashem after what happened, if they were continuing to hope that Leon would return. But now that he knew they had been manticore hunters all along, he realized that it was not hope that kept them there, but revenge.

"Don't speak of things you know nothing of," his father's voice was eerily calm. "You are hardly doing your brother any favors by questioning your duty."

"But if he's still out there, we can save him! We can bring him home!"

"He isn't!" No sooner had his father interrupted him, than he looked shocked at having spoken.

"What do you mean…he isn't?" Sasha was afraid of the answer.

"Forget what I said, Sasha," his father turned back towards the door, but Sasha grasped his arm before he could touch the door handle.

"Answer me, father! What did you mean? Where is Leon?"

Sasha had never been more terrified than he did at that moment. Time slowed down as his father turned around to face him, and a cold sweat broke out on his brow.

"Leon died, son."

Purple spots danced in front of Sasha's eyes, and he felt dizzy.

"When?" he couldn't even hear his own voice, and for a moment, doubted whether or not he had truly spoken.

"Not two years after he escaped from the boarding school," his father's voice was starting to sound garbled to his ears. "He came back, and was seen stinging a child belonging to a Grusrecian baron. As if whatever manticore that stung him wasn't enough, he had to go after an innocent child. He was only twelve and yet he had already become a monster."

"Don't..." Sasha began, but was unsure of what to say. Don't what? Don't talk about him that way? Don't continue with the story? Though it pained him to hear his father talk about his brother the same way he talked of any other manticore, he couldn't bring himself to finish the sentence. He had to hear the rest of what his father had to say.

"He was caught and brought to the palace, and your mother and I were summoned to say goodbye to him before he was fed to the flames. Now Sasha, you must make a decision. Do you want those manticores down in the dungeon to live to steal more of our children, or would you rather they burned where they stand?" His father, who had told the story with a completely neutral face expression, finally allowed fury to show in his gaze.

Sasha couldn't bring himself to speak.

"Any of those manticores, including your Ydana, could easily sting another child one day. It could even be your child they take from you."

"Any children I have with Princess Sahar are likely to be born manticores, let's not forget."

"Princess Sahar may have been stung by a manticore, but she has overcome that, and is as human as you or I," his father said.

Sasha thought he sounded insane, but couldn't possibly explain to him that Princess Sahar was as much of a manticore as Ydana or any other. All his parents were concerned about was Sasha marrying into the royal family.

"Any child stung by a manticore would not have been happy as a human," Sasha's voice came out as a whisper. "That's the point of them being stung. Otherwise, the stinger would kill them. You should know that as well as I do."

He wanted to point out that he was engaged to a manticore, but knew that Princess Sahar was hardly an example of a manticore who was happier that way.

"Perhaps they would not be happy as humans, but they would be safe," his father turned towards the door. "Not like your brother."

Too shocked even for tears, Sasha simply watched his father turn the door handle and leave him standing in the hallway. When the door closed behind his father, Sasha realized how truly alone he was.

## CHAPTER TWENTY-TWO

Ydana's back was sticky with sweat, and she heard the sound of a fire roaring close behind her. She did not need to open her eyes to see that her feet were not touching the ground and her hands were tied behind her back.

"This is your last chance, Valida," Mitra's voice made Ydana open her eyes. The terrible woman's pupils were so narrow in the light from the flames, that it looked as if she had none. "Will you join me, or will you die?"

Looking around, Ydana found Val next to her, chains circling her and tying her arms behind her. She was hanging from the end of a chain, which must have been the same way Ydana hung. She struggled to look upwards at the ceiling, only to find that the other end of the chain was up so high that it disappeared into darkness. There was no sign of Soheila and the others, and Ydana hoped they were alright.

"I've already told you that I would never join you," Val's voice sounded from close by. "And if you think I would believe that you'd let me have that chance, you are mistaken."

"Then this is where we part ways," Mitra said dryly. "I look forward to watching you burn. I'm sure those parents of yours won't be looking forward to such a thing, however. I'm giving you the most painful death I can, because you will know while you are burning, that your parents have to see it and your true love is burning beside you."

It was then that Ydana looked around for the other manticores, and, straining her ears, she picked up their muffled cries through a barred window on the opposite wall. In that moment, she hated Mitra more than ever. It was bad enough that she wanted Val dead for something she had no control over, but what she was doing to Vash and Soheila was even worse.

"Let Ydana live," Val tugged at the chains that bound her wrists. "You may want me dead, but your quarrel is not with her. She wasn't even alive yet when you were stung. She has nothing to do with this."

As Ydana faced Val, she felt the heat of the flames on one side of her face.

"I can't let you do that, Val. Even when the fire consumes us, I won't leave you."

When Val met her eyes, her face lost its strained expression, and she actually smiled, much to Ydana's surprise. It was then that she knew that a life without Val was no life at all.

"That's awfully sweet of you, but if I have so much as a chance to let you live, I have to take it."

"You two make me sick," Mitra turned away and began walking to the door, where one of her men waited. "Good riddance."

When Mitra stood illuminated in the doorway, the man next to her knelt to the ground and pulled a wooden lever. There was a screech, and to Ydana's horror, the chains holding her and Val up from the ground began moving backwards. She barely had time to register that the man who had pulled the lever was Sasha, and in that moment, she hated him.

Stealing a glance behind her, Ydana could not help but gasp at the wall of flame.

## CHAPTER TWENTY-THREE

"Val!" Ydana could hardly hear herself above the rattling of chains and the roar of the bonfire. She struggled to change into a manticore, but could feel that the flames were too close to her to allow her to transform.

"I can't transform," Val said with a groan. Her dark hair hung in front of her face, slick with sweat.

In a panic, Ydana struggled against the chains, swaying from side to side as she hovered above the ground. She even tried to reach the ground with her feet, to slow her down, looking all around her for something, anything, to grab ahold of.

Suddenly, her chain was yanked to a still position. She looked up just in time to see a figure hacking at the chain again and again, until she fell down, her face against the cold stone.

"Get out of here, Ydana," Sasha hauled her to her feet. "Please run away while you still can. You can fly if you…hey!"

Ydana had no time to thank him as she ran towards Val, grasping at the chains that bound her.

"Ydana, just save yourself before it's too late!" Sasha ran after her.

Taking manticore form, she bit at the chain that held Val up, before swinging her tail into it. The heat from the bonfire grew hotter, and she struggled to stay in manticore form as she gripped the chain in her teeth, placing all four paws firmly onto the ground. But all of the strength she possessed was not enough. She and Val were still moving towards the bonfire.

"Forget the others, Ydana, just get away while you still can!"

"What is wrong with you, Sasha?" Ydana turned to him, still in manticore form, but allowing only her face to take human shape. She could tell that this form scared him. "You just broke my chain, why can't you break hers?"

"She's a manticore," Sasha stammered as he tried to cling to Ydana's leg.

"So am I!" Ydana swung her tail at him, stinging him in the shoulder. He cried out in pain.

Taking half-human form to snatch the sword he had dropped, Ydana didn't even give Sasha a backwards glance as he crumpled to the ground. Though she heard commotion from behind her and was sure she would be shot at any moment, she didn't dare hesitate.

Fire Consumes Us

Swinging the sword against Val's chain again and again, she felt tears spring to her eyes. She knew she was only ruining the sword further than Sasha already had by cutting through one chain, and that was hardly helping her free Val. Shots rang out, but she couldn't stop. Eventually, she dropped the sword and tried, in vain, to unlink the chains. Her fingers bled, but she couldn't stop.

"Save the others," Val croaked. "It's too late for me."

"No!" Ydana cried. "I don't want to live without you!"

From behind her, a roar sounded. She spun around, bracing herself to face Mitra. But it was not Mitra who stood before her.

Sasha, getting to his feet, had black fur sprouting from all over his body, before he crouched down on four paws, birdlike wings sprouting from his back. Facing the manticore hunters, he snarled.

Swallowing her surprise at Sasha's transformation, Ydana yanked again, hopelessly, at Val's chains. Too close to the fire to both stay there and keep from reverting back to human form, Ydana flew up towards the ceiling instead. To her surprise, she found not a ceiling, but an open hole for the smoke to flow through. It had only appeared dark because it was nighttime again. Ydana could just barely make out the glimmer of stars through the thick smoke that floated above her.

The other end of Val's chain was looped over a pole near the top of the opening, and held in place with a hook. Ydana knew that Val's weight at the other end would make it difficult to lift the hook over the pole, and instead looked around for what was pulling the pole towards the fire. On one wall, she found a gear that was turning. If she could stop it in its tracks, Val would not move any closer to the fire.

Taking on her half-human form, she looked around for something, anything, to put in between the teeth of the gear. It was then that she remembered the small knife at her neck. Taking off the necklace, she jabbed the knife, sheath and all, into the gear, and prayed that it would hold just long enough.

Everything screeched to a halt, the gears straining against the knife wedged between them. But a scream from below made Ydana look down. Though she had stopped moving any closer, Val was right next to the fire, and was burning. It was too late.

## CHAPTER TWENTY-FOUR

Ydana felt as if she would faint. Below her was Val, screaming in pain as she burned, and there was nothing she could do. Her wings felt weak, and she perched herself on the pole, grasping Val's chain with both hands and pulling at it uselessly.

With no warning, several manticores flew, one by one, through the opening and right over Ydana's head. She flattened herself against the pole as best she could and watched them dive below her towards the manticore hunters. Some of them, in half-human form, carried weapons. One of them jabbed his spear into the chain repeatedly, letting Val crumple to the ground, while a group of at least ten carried vases and pots, pouring enough water over the bonfire to put it out, save for a few embers.

Dropping to the ground below, Ydana spread her wings as she landed, scooping Val up in both arms and carrying her a short distance away from the fire.

"Val, stay with me," she begged. "Transform! Now! Quickly!"

She was barely conscious, and Ydana was not sure if Val had heard her, but as she transformed, she healed, and her strength began to come back.

Looking up, Ydana saw Tara at the front of this manticore horde, shooting arrow after arrow into the manticore hunters. Behind her came the Ruling Lady, spear in hand, who appeared to think nothing of thrusting her weapon into hunter after hunter.

By the time Val transformed, she was able to stand on four legs, with only minimal burns on her body. The few burns there were rapidly closing. Ydana sighed in relief before taking manticore form and bounding after her.

Catching sight of Sasha, laying on the ground in human form once more, Ydana stopped in her tracks. He must have been shot with one of the manticore hunters' special weapons. Taking his shirt between her teeth, as if carrying a cub by the scruff, she continued flying.

As they flew past a corridor that looked deserted, Ydana placed Sasha in the open doorway of an empty room. It was a safe place to heal, and she owed him at least that much after he had saved her, and after she had turned him into a manticore. The fact that he had forgotten all about Val and the others made her less inclined to help him, but she would not leave him in the middle of the battle, defenseless.

That done, she found Val grasping a manticore hunter in her mouth and throwing him down the hall, as two others looked on, terrified. All Ydana had to do was snarl at them, and they ran away.

"Where did they take my parents?" Val took the same form Ydana had earlier, transforming only her face while the rest of her stayed in manticore form.

The manticore hunter was too terrified to speak, and Ydana growled what she hoped sounded like she wanted Val to hurry. When Val followed, her features melding back into a lionlike face, Ydana took half-human form and shouted to her.

"What is that form that only changes our faces? It happened to me while I was trying to save you."

"I have only taken that form a few times," Val took half-human form to answer. "We have to be very angry, and it is a very difficult form to call up at will."

Taking manticore form again, Val let out a roar that shook the ground. From far away came a roar that sounded like Soheila. Ydana was not sure when she had begun to differentiate each manticore's roar, but she felt proud of herself for having recognized Soheila's voice.

Flying up a large spiral staircase, Ydana and Val soon found Vash, Soheila, Vaja, Dara and Misty each being led by a manticore hunter, their wrists and ankles tied. Next to them, a scowl on her face, stood Mitra.

"Not only do you steal Sasha from me, but you come for my prisoners as well? I won't let you leave this place alive!"

As Mitra finished her sentence, she took manticore form, making the last word sound more like a growl than speech. She leaped at them the moment she transformed, but Ydana and Val were ready for her, meeting her in mid-leap.

Ydana's first move was to bite Mitra in the face as hard as she could, to keep her from biting Val. But Mitra lashed out with her tail, the stinger catching Ydana in the shoulder. Flapping her feathered wings madly, Mitra threw Ydana off of her, but Val immediately took her place, and began clawing Mitra in the stomach with all four paws. Leaping up, Ydana gripped Mitra's wing in her jaws, but only succeeded in ripping out a mouthful of feathers.

Spitting the feathers out, she glanced back down at the imprisoned manticores. Soheila was jumping up to slam her head into a manticore hunter's nose. Her hands still bound in front of her, she took the manticore hunter's crossbow from his belt and held it up, ready to fire.

Next to her, Vash and the others took advantage of the manticore hunters' surprise and found various ways to incapacitate them. Vash skillfully dropped to the ground and kicked his captor's legs out from under him. Even with his wrists and ankles tied, he was fast. Though he could not grab his captor's weapon, he put enough body weight on him to keep him from drawing it himself.

Misty had a harder time, as she was no skilled fighter, but she attempted to copy Soheila and slam her head into the manticore hunter's nose. She hurt herself in the process, but it was enough to distract the man.

Before Soheila could fire the weapon, Ydana placed all four of her paws against the wall, using it to launch herself at Val and Mitra. She plowed into Val, knocking her away. In that moment, with the clearest shot at Mitra she could get, Soheila fired the crossbow and was immediately seized by the hunter from whom she had stolen it.

Crumpling to the ground, Mitra gripped her shoulder, human once more. Ydana and Val immediately flew at the manticore hunters, batting them aside with their massive paws and letting loose loud roars that echoed throughout the hall.

No sooner had Soheila's weapon been wrenched out of her hand, than it lay on the ground beside the unconscious manticore hunter. Before long, they had all either been knocked out cold or chased away, Val landing in front of the last one and taking human form to punch him in the face.

Not even waiting to make sure the hunter fell to the ground, Val took manticore form, leaped across the room, and took human form again faster than Ydana had ever seen her do. As soon as Mitra tried to stand up, still pressing her hand to her shoulder, Val gripped her by the front of her dress, making her stand up.

"How dare you!" Mitra snarled at Val. "Let me go!"

"How dare *I*? How dare *you*!" Val hissed. "You tried to kill me!"

"Like you tried to kill me all those years ago?" Mitra raised an eyebrow. "How does it feel, Valida, for the shoe to be on the other foot?"

"It isn't!" Val sounded unsure.

"Take us to the Podishah or this knife will go into your neck," Vaja pressed the point of a knife she had found on one of the manticore hunters into Mitra's neck. "You'll take an awfully long time to heal from that. We don't know how long, as I don't think a manticore has been stabbed in the head before, so it could be years."

Mitra visibly shivered. Ydana guessed she had never been at the end of one of her own weapons before. As Vaja urged her forward with the point of the weapon, Mitra led them forward without another word.

Soon, they heard shouting, and the clang of swords, from up ahead, and everyone but Misty, Vaja and Mitra ran down the hall. Throwing the massive doors open, Ydana was surprised to see more manticores than she had expected, fighting against the human guards that surrounded the Podishah.

Bow in hand, Tara shot arrow after arrow, most of which clanged against armor, but some of which found their marks. The Ruling Lady soared across the room to thrust her spear into the throat of one manticore hunter, who looked to be aiming a crossbow at the newcomers. He dropped to the ground dead before he could loose the bolt. Another manticore hunter spilled a large pot full of something, at the same time as another hurled a flaming candle into the puddle.

Ydana cried out as flames erupted from the spilled liquid, right in front of the Ruling Lady, who went up in flames and disappeared completely. Hands shaking, Ydana covered her mouth. Until that moment, it had not occurred to her that she had never before seen a manticore die. She and Val had been threatened with death, yet she had not completely realized what that meant.

Leaping over her, Soheila launched a bolt from the manticore hunter weapon she still held, which found its mark in the throat of the manticore hunter who had lit the Ruling Lady on fire. Though Soheila did not look visibly distraught at her mother's abrupt death, Ydana saw briefly that there were tears spilling down her cheeks.

Tara's cheeks looked wet with tears as well, and her aim was less true with every arrow she shot, as if the tears were blurring her vision. This surprised Ydana, as she had thought that the Ruling Lady had barely remembered Tara.

As the manticores continued to fight, fewer and fewer of them ventured anywhere near the flames that were still there, in the middle of the room. No other manticores burned, though two of the guards were shoved into the fire, to be pulled quickly out by their comrades.

Behind her, Val was stepping forward to help, but stopped. Ydana turned around to see Vash place a hand on his daughter's shoulder. She didn't hear what Vash whispered to Val, but whatever it was stopped Val in her tracks. All Ydana could do was stand there, as Vash stepped into the room.

"He wants to fight the Podishah himself," Val whispered into her ear. "He says we can't interfere."

"Does he think the Podishah won't allow anyone to interfere?" Ydana gritted her teeth. "Because I don't think he cares as much as your father does about being fair. He can't even take manticore form right now!"

"Believe me, Ydana, I'm prepared to step in if I have to," Val whispered.

Ydana gasped as Vash simply stopped in front of the sea of battling manticores. She braced herself to attack, fully expecting the manticore hunters, or the guards to notice him. But they were all busy losing to the manticores.

Seeing what Vash was doing, Soheila picked up a fallen sword and brought it to him. Taking it from her, he held it high, pointing its tip at the ceiling.

"I challenge the Podishah to single combat!" he cried.

"Who are you to make such a demand?" came the Podishah's voice. "You're nothing but a man-eating beast."

The Podishah looked older than Ydana had pictured him. She had only ever seen him in passing, and years ago at that, barely remembering what he looked like. His grey hair almost reached his shoulders, and matched the silver of his tunic so that he looked almost ethereal. As he stared at Vash, the eyes of the few other nobles, the guards, and the manticores, followed in the same direction. The battle had ceased.

"My name is Vashar Khan Jamshidi," Vash began. Several people gasped, as they knew the Jamshidi family was the one who the current ruling family had overthrown.

"Seize him!" the Podishah pointed to Vash.

Before the guards could do more than take a single step forward, Ydana and Val leaped into the room in manticore form to stand on either side of Vash, growling.

"I was heir to the throne, and that was stolen from me when I became a manticore," Vash continued.

"Because no one wants an immortal ruler," the Podishah said, "and they never will."

"And yet our kind has always had an immortal ruler," Vash did not lower his sword.

"Having an immortal ruler is fine for a small population like yours, but you can't run a country that way," Lord Warrington spoke up.

Until then, Ydana had not realized that Sasha's father was even in the room. He hardly seemed like someone who would lift a finger in battle, and was hardly dressed for it either.

"We have you surrounded," Vash reminded the room. "Either fight me in single combat, or elect someone else to do it for you."

As if to remind the Podishah just how high the stakes were, every manticore in the room, whether currently sporting a human face or a lion one, bared their teeth at the guards they had cornered.

"Fine," the Podishah stood up. "Seeing as only a manticore can best a manticore in single combat, I choose Princess Sahar."

Heads turned to look around the room, before Mitra muttered a "very well" and stepped forward, brushing Vaja's dagger away from her. Ydana wondered why Mitra was not admitting to having been shot and rendered unable to return to manticore form. Though Vash was equally stuck in human form, which hardly anyone else in the room knew, what made Mitra think she could win? Even if the effect of the manticore blood solution wore off, Vash would shed its effects first. She couldn't help but feel as if Mitra was up to something.

Making her way around Vash to stand in front of him, Mitra held her hand out to a nearby guard, expectantly. The guard quickly handed her his sword before stepping back again. Vash nodded to Ydana, and she and Val reluctantly stepped backwards the way they had come.

Mitra was the first to strike, jumping forward with the point of her sword out towards Vash. But Vash would not be caught unawares. He easily stepped aside and tripped her so that she fell face first into the ground. But before her nose hit the floor, she dropped her sword and, miraculously, stood up on four paws.

A collective gasp arose from the spectators. If Ydana had been in human form, she would have gasped as well.

"But we saw her be shot with one of the same weapons they used on us," Misty's voice was barely audible from behind Ydana. "How could she have already recovered?"

It was then that Ydana realized that with how many years Mitra had spent working with manticore hunter weapons, she had to have become close to immune. She had been playing them, pretending to be stuck in human form for longer than she really was.

Before Ydana's eyes, Vash went from the picture of confidence, to surprised. Though he held his sword out in front of him and didn't let a scared expression take over his features, his gaze anxiously darted around as he struggled to decide where to run every time Mitra pounced after him.

Bracing herself to pounce in between the two, Ydana was taken aback when Val growled quietly at her. It was then that she understood how terribly her interference would ruin the fight, even if the fight she was witnessing was nothing close to fair.

Taking a look around the large room, she noticed that Soheila was watching, helpless as Vash dodged Mitra's attacks again and again, growing weaker and more tired every time. Tara, still in the air with an arrow trained on the Podishah, simply looked sad. Any attack against Mitra, to spare Vash, would only undermine what Vash was trying to do, far more than his death would.

Ydana was still feeling at a loss for what to do, when suddenly, another manticore flew above her head to land in front of Vash, tackling Mitra just as she was about to pounce, and gripping her by the neck. Defeated, Mitra stepped back, and the newcomer took human form again, revealing Sasha. Ydana almost didn't recognize him with his darkened hair and green catlike eyes. Turning human again, Mitra gasped, as did most of the spectators.

Finding Lord Warrington near the Podishah, Ydana noticed for the first time that Sasha's mother was with him, and now buried her face in her husband's shoulder.

"My son is no manticore," Sasha's father was saying. "This is some sort of trick!"

"It's no trick, father," Sasha extended a hand and helped Mitra to her feet. "I was stung during the fight, and if I had not been meant to become a manticore, I would simply have died. I much prefer this outcome, and I hope that you will agree with me that a manticore for a son is better than a dead one. Don't make the same mistake you did before."

This resulted in more chatter around the room. Ydana knew what Sasha meant by his reference to a mistake made before, but his brother becoming a manticore was not common knowledge.

"No son of mine is a manticore," Lord Warrington said over the noise of the many hushed voices.

"What am I to do about it, father, if you won't have a manticore for a son? Hide, the way some of our kind do? No, I believe in a world in which we can embrace our manticore nature."

Next, Sasha did something that truly surprised Ydana. He turned his back on the Podishah and his father, and bowed to Vash. Ydana looked towards Lord and Lady Warrington again, whose expressions of surprise deepened to include shame and utter disbelief.

"Seize them!" Soheila called to the manticores, taking advantage of the distraction. No sooner had she spoken, than Tara and two other archers fired arrow after arrow into each of the guards, before Tara pointed her last one straight at the Podishah.

The battle resumed, but with far less fighting from the humans, who were each either killed immediately or held at swordpoint until ropes could be tied around their wrists.

Soheila picked up the sword that Mitra had dropped, and slashed Mitra's arm with it to make her unable to take manticore form again. That done, she kicked Mitra to the ground, pressing the point of the sword to her throat.

"Wait!" Sasha ran to Soheila, who did not look up from Mitra's terrified face. Ydana did not hear Soheila's reply, if there was one, and her gaze stayed exactly where it was.

Another manticore tackled the Podishah's brother and held him down with a massive paw, teeth poised for attack.

"Would you surrender?" Vash strode confidently through the middle of the room towards the Podishah, Val taking human form to walk behind him. "Or would you rather die, along with your entire family, the way my family did at the hands of yours?"

Lifting her head to snarl at a guard who dared take one step toward Vash, Ydana spotted a familiar face hiding behind a few dead bodies. The Podishah's own daughter, Zahra, grew wide-eyed when Ydana's gaze met hers.

"Fine, kill me if you must," the Podishah was saying, as Ydana suspected he would. It was too difficult for most people to let go of their pride.

Leaping up into the air, Ydana barely touched the ground on the other side of the room before picking Zahra up in her mouth and turning back around. As she came to stand next to Vash again, she closed her jaws just enough to make the girl scream as Ydana's teeth sank into her stomach and back. She wanted the Podishah to see that his daughter was in pain, for little else would make him surrender. If he did not, could Ydana truly bite an innocent girl in half? A girl who she had once played with as a child? She would have to.

"Wait," the Podishah allowed a slight amount of panic to show on his face, though he was clearly trying not to show how afraid he was.

Though Ydana doubted that her fellow manticores knew who the Podishah's relatives were, she guessed that Vash understood that they had a bargaining chip in the girl who Ydana had flown across the room to capture.

The Podishah looked alarmed, but only for a moment.

"I need your word that no one will be harmed," he kept his voice calm, though Ydana suspected he felt anything but. "Whatever the word of manticores is worth."

"You have my word," Vash nodded. "No one will come to any harm. Every human present will be held in the dungeon briefly while we sort out other arrangements."

"Seize the humans," Soheila all but roared as she transformed to her half-human form, the poison evidently having worn off.

Every manticore who was able to transform took half-human form and pointed weapons at the humans closest to them. As each human in the room was stripped of their weapons and led away by the manticores, Mitra transformed, flying up through the skylight so quickly that it took Ydana a moment to register what she had seen. Only a moment passed before Sasha flew up after her.

Changing to half-human form, Ydana hauled Zahra to her feet. Beside her, Val tore a piece of fabric from her shirt and used it to bind the princess' hands together.

"How can you do this, you despicable manticore," Zahra's voice was hoarse. It was shocking to Ydana that a girl she had spent so much time with as a child, even if it was at both of their mothers' insistence, could speak to cruelly to her.

"I'm just glad I can keep you alive. I didn't want to kill you," Ydana left out the fact that she had not been sure she could have killed Zahra.

"I need to go after Mitra," Val whispered.

"Let me do it," Ydana said. "Mitra has no personal problem with me, so maybe I can reason with her."

For a moment, she was afraid that Val would object, but instead, Val nodded and shoved Zahra forward towards the other humans who were being led away.

## CHAPTER TWENTY-FIVE

Once outside, floating above the palace, Sasha turned his head back to make sure he had not been followed, though he doubted that he would be missed. It was unlikely that the manticores trusted him enough to let him help anyway, especially considering that his parents were among the prisoners, however briefly.

Looking ahead of him once more, he spotted Princess Sahar flying away, silhouetted against the sun. With a roar, he flapped his wings to catch up to her, but she only flew faster. As he chased her, he looked around him at the scenery, surprised to find himself so high up in the air.

"What is it you want?" she took half-human form to shout back at him. "Are you here to gloat?"

Sasha could only roar and shake his head. If only he could take the form she did so that he could talk to her. All he could seem to do was fly after her until she either outflew him or gave up and stopped.

Evidently, she realized the same thing, and dove back down to the ground. As he dove after her, Sasha was certain that she was trying to outrun him, until she spread her wings and glided towards one of the floating islands in the sky.

"Was it your plan all along?" she shouted at him the moment she landed. "Or were you so determined not to marry me, that you helped the manticores overthrow my family?"

Sasha took human form before his feet even touched the ground, and he stumbled in the dirt.

"I still want to marry you," he stood up, brushing the dirt from his trousers.

"But I'm hardly a princess anymore," Sahar protested. "Your parents won't care about me."

"So that's it?" Sasha stared her down as she took human form, shrinking to the same height as him. "You're not a princess, and you think I don't care about you as a person? Whether you are Sahar or…or Mitra means nothing to me. I never would have agreed to marry you if I didn't think I would care about you. The real you."

Mitra, for he would refer to her as her real name, simply stood, silent, waiting for him to say more.

"Mitra, I already never cared when I found out that you were a manticore," Sasha surprised himself by using her given name. "And now that I am one, too, I think I'm allowed to decide things for myself without listening to my parents."

"You're just scared to be a manticore," Mitra said. "And you think you need my help."

"I may be intimidated," Sasha grasped her hands in his, "but I'm not scared. In fact, I'm happy to be a manticore. If we have both been granted an exceptionally long life, should we not spend it together?"

"Manticore or not, I'll be exiled," Mitra pointed out. "I doubt I will be able to come back to Hashem without being attacked the moment I fly across the mountains."

"Then I will come with you," Sasha placed a hand to Mitra's face and planted a kiss on her lips.

Though they had been betrothed for nearly a month, Sasha and Mitra had never kissed, and it surprised him how different this was from when he had kissed Ydana. He had kissed his friend knowing that it would be the only time, and hoping, even, that she would find happiness without him. But the moment he shared with Mitra was only the beginning of a life he would have with her.

It took Ydana a moment to catch up to Mitra and Sasha, seeing as they were well away from the skylight by the time Ydana flew after them. She flew over the nearby floating islands looking for them, finally spotting them standing on top of one, in human form. To her amazement, they were kissing. Gliding down, she landed on the ground nearby, landing in her human form.

"Ydana, don't arrest her!" Sasha stood protectively in front of Mitra.

"I hardly need help against her, Sasha," Mitra protested.

"There's no need to take her back there, I swear it," Sasha did not move.

"I don't know how much I can trust you, after you refused to save Val from the fire, Sasha," Ydana glared at him. "But I will hear your argument for why I shouldn't take her back with me."

Mitra rolled her eyes. "First of all, there are two of us, and only one of you. Besides, Sasha honestly wants to help me live as a manticore…with him."

Ydana looked from Mitra's face to Sasha's. "You're still…marrying him?"

"Well, I don't suppose there will be an actual marriage, per se, seeing as I'm no doubt exiled," Mitra frowned, "but we do plan to stay together."

"You see? Mitra has only just begun to actually live as a manticore," Sasha continued to stand in front of Mitra no matter how much she tried to push him aside. "Don't arrest her now that she's finally not a threat to you. I promise, we're leaving."

Stealing a glance back the way she had come, Ydana sighed. "Fine. But don't try coming back to Hashem. And that includes the manticore island, or what's left of it. Hopefully I can beg Vash not to exile you, Sasha, seeing as you helped us."

"I won't be coming back."

"In a few years, your parents will come around, and they will want to see you after all. And besides, don't you need to at least go home and pack? You can't just leave with no food or clothes at all."

"What we do is none of your concern," Sasha frowned. Ydana suspected that he had thought of exactly that, but did not want her to know that he was planning to return home and pack.

"Fine, don't go home and pack," Ydana said. "I'll say that you both overpowered me and flew away."

"Thank you, Ydana," Sasha came forward and embraced her. She was too surprised to move.

"Good luck," she said once Sasha returned to Mitra's side.

Both of them took their manticore forms at once, and flew away. Ydana watched them until they were obscured by clouds.

## CHAPTER TWENTY-SIX

No sooner had Ydana landed on her parents' rooftop, than she heard Val roaring her name. As Val soared down from the sky to land in front of her, Ydana took human form for the first time all day, her bare feet touching the warm roof tiles.

"Where have you been all day?" Val transformed and embraced her. "I was worried. I wasn't sure if you had been captured somehow, or if you had…left for good."

"I'm sorry," she buried her face in Val's shoulder. "With everything that happened, I needed to get away."

"I understand, you don't have to explain if you don't want to."

Ydana hoped that Val wouldn't ask about Mitra and Sasha.

"If anyone asks, we'll say you tried to stop them and they flew away," Val said.

Eyes wide, Ydana ended the embrace, looking up into her face.

"I know you, Ydana," Val smirked. "And that princess you were concerned about, Zahra, is fine. We're allowing most of the former royals to live in the same areas of the palace they had before. I don't think she cared about the throne once she realized that we wouldn't be changing anything for the worse. Her father and uncle are just upset not to be in power, but I'm sure they will be fine, eventually."

"Ydana, is that you?" a familiar voice called from down below.

Rolling her eyes, Ydana turned away to look down from the roof. Victor stood on the ground, shielding his eyes from the sun as he looked up. Jumping down from the roof, Ydana and Val took half-human form to float to the ground, landing on human feet once more. Victor jumped backwards, surprised at what he had seen.

"How did…and what sort of uncivilized clothing are you wearing? I can see your stomach! Mother and father will not be pleased. And you, whoever you are!" he turned to Val. "You cannot possibly call that a shirt, either!"

Val adjusted her clothing the best she could before holding a hand out to Victor. "You must be Ydana's brother. I'm Val."

"I will not shake hands with a manticore!"

"You will," Lord Azra stepped around the corner to join them. "We have heard about everything that happened. Your mother is none too happy about the manticores making the kingdom theirs, but I'm sure she will realize that not much will change for us. I'm just glad you're alright, and that there will be fewer manticore hunters."

With a smile, Ydana embraced her father.

"How can you…" Victor began, before Azra turned to glare at his stepson.

"You do realize that this means you can come home any time," Azra added, "and your mother and brother can't have a problem with that."

"Or you could live in the palace," Val offered. "I doubt too many manticores are going to live indoors. There is plenty of room for humans."

"Thank you for the offer," Azra looked at Val. "I'm sure Ydana's mother would actually be happy about that. I don't believe I got your name."

"Val," Val shook Azra's hand. "And I'm sorry…"

"Don't be," Azra interrupted, and Ydana wondered if he had guessed that Val was apologizing for stinging her and did not want to hear about it. "Just promise me that you two will come back once Ylaine is less distraught over current events."

With a promise that they would return, Ydana and Val flew away again, through a sky that was nearly as full of manticores as their island had been. Soon, they flew past a small floating island, where a girl sat on the edge, drawing patterns in the dirt with a small stick. Though her curly hair hid her face, Ydana recognized Tara immediately.

Roaring Tara's name, Ydana flew to her, Val beside her. As she looked up at them, they took human form and sat down next to her.

"Are you alright?" Val put an arm around his best friend.

"Just fine," Tara picked up her stick and continued drawing patterns in the ground. "I just…killed people, is all. And the Ruling Lady is gone."

"There continues to be a Ruling Lady," Val said, unsmiling. "But yes, my grandmother is gone, after centuries of existence. But perhaps she has gone to join my grandfather. At least that's how I prefer to think about it."

"She saved me, when the manticore hunters attacked the island," Tara said. "I didn't think she had even remembered who I was, or cared at all if I lived or died, but she purposely flew in between me and one of the manticore hunters' harpoons. Even though it took her such a long time to heal, because she is so much older than we are."

"She was truly amazing," Val agreed, "and I hope my parents and, in a very, very long time, I myself, will do a great job of filling her shoes."

"It's still not fair that she had to die the way she did," Tara clutched the stick in her hand, before flinging it over the side of the island. "It's just not fair!"

"It's not," Ydana agreed. "But we should remember that she helped us build a world in which fewer people will hunt manticores, where we can live amongst humans as if we're hardly different. My father didn't even care anymore that I'm a manticore, because he has no reason to. And my brother was more shocked about my clothing than my transforming right in front of his eyes."

"This is true," Val agreed. "Everything that happened was not in vain."

Ydana looked up at the manticores that dotted the sky.

—The End

ABOUT THE AUTHOR

A.R. Hellbender is half Persian, grew up in the San Francisco Bay Area before making her way up the west coast. She lives in Washington with her husband, dog and three cats. Her other works include Unicorn Hunting and Unicorn Revenge. When not writing or reading, she can be found drawing fantasy art or playing bass with her metal band.

Made in the USA
Middletown, DE
27 January 2025